"Would you care to put away your whiskey and cards for a few minutes and hear from God's Word?"

The place grew quiet. Deadly quiet. Then several tipped chairs dropped to all fours with the crack of a rifle shot.

He studied each and every face. The hardened men, the eager boys who probably shaved once a week, the anxious greenhorns and—

He stared. A woman. A young woman. A very pretty young woman who flashed him a bold grin. Not the sort of woman who frequented saloons. No tight, revealing bodice, no rouged cheeks. From what he could see as she sat behind a table, she wore a tanned leather vest. A battered cowboy hat hung down her back. Her sorrel-colored hair was bound in a braid as thick as a woman's wrist.

He jerked his gaze away but three faces away it returned to her. She leaned her elbows on the table and regarded him as steadily as he did her. Not the least bit ladylike at all. And yet. . . yet. . .he felt trapped by her insolent beauty.

What was she doing in here? What sort of town opened their saloon to women? Apart from the usual crude types? Right then and there he knew he had his job cut out for him.

LINDA FORD and her husband raised a family of fourteen children, ten adopted, providing her plenty of opportunity to experience God's love and faithfulness. One of her goals in writing is to reveal a little of God's wondrous love through the lives of the people in her stories. She lives in Alberta, Canada, on a ranch she shares with her husband, a paraplegic client, boomerang children, and adorable visiting grandchildren.

Books by Linda Ford

Glory and the Rawhide Preacher

Linda Ford

Heartsong Presents

To the faithful Heartsong Presents readers. You have read our stories. You have commented on them. Most of all, I hope you have enjoyed them. Thank You.

A note from the Author:
I love to hear from my readers! You may correspond with me by writing:

Linda Ford
Author Relations
PO Box 721
Uhrichsville, OH 44683

ISBN 978-1-61626-576-2

GLORY AND THE RAWHIDE PREACHER

All scripture is taken from the King James Version of the Bible.

This book is a work of fiction. Names, characters, places, and incidents are either products of the author's imagination or used fictitiously.

Our mission is to publish and distribute inspirational products offering exceptional value and biblical encouragement to the masses.

PRINTED IN THE U.S.A.

one

*Bonners Ferry, Idaho, during the Kootenai gold rush,
Spring 1864*

His name was Levi. Levi Powers. Twenty-six years of age. A man intent on fulfilling his vow. He pulled to a halt in front of the saloon, tugged his worn cowboy hat low on his head, and swung from the back of his mount, landing neatly on his feet. This was where he intended to start.

His boots thudded on the wooden sidewalk in front of the swinging doors. He strode inside, grabbed a chair, stood on it, and called, "Would you care to put away your whiskey and cards for a few minutes and hear from God's Word?"

The place grew quiet. Deadly quiet. Then several tipped chairs dropped to all fours with the crack of a rifle shot.

He studied each and every face. The hardened men, the eager boys who probably shaved once a week, the anxious greenhorns, and—

He stared. A woman. A young woman. A very pretty young woman who flashed him a bold grin. Not the sort of woman who frequented saloons. No tight, revealing bodice. No rouged cheeks. From what he could see as she sat behind a table, she wore a tanned leather vest. A battered cowboy hat hung down her back. Her sorrel-colored hair was bound in a braid as thick as a woman's wrist.

He jerked his gaze away, but three faces away it returned to her. She leaned her elbows on the table and regarded him as steadily as he did her. Not the least bit ladylike at all. And yet. . .yet. . .he felt trapped by her insolent beauty.

What was she doing in here? What sort of town opened its saloon to women? Apart from the usual crude types? Right then and there he knew he had his job cut out for him.

He forced his attention away from her, angled his body so he wasn't able to look directly at her, and opened the Bible. He had long thought about the words he would say when he found the place where he would start his work. And yet he paused, momentarily forgetting his plan.

Thankfully the pages fell open at the chosen place. "I'm reading from the Gospel of John, chapter ten, verse ten, where Jesus says, 'I am come that they might have life, and that they might have it more abundantly.' My name is Levi Powers, and I am here to tell you about this abundant life Jesus offers. I'll be available anytime, day or night, if you want to talk. Otherwise, I will be walking the streets, stopping where I see people and telling them the good news. And Sundays, I'll hold services."

One bleary-eyed patron raised a hand. "Mister Preacher, where you gonna hold these here services? Ain't no church." He gave what Levi expected was supposed to be a laugh, but it sounded more like a choked sigh.

"I'll preach in a field until I find suitable quarters for a church." He closed his Bible, signifying he was done.

The room was quiet. Someone coughed. Slowly the noise grew, though not to the deafening level it had been when he stepped inside. He understood his presence made some of them uncomfortable, and he strode toward the door, allowing his gaze to slide to the woman, rest there only a second before he schooled it away. Not the sort of woman a preacher man should be admiring.

She nodded briefly as if acknowledging his thoughts, then pushed her chair back and rose.

He hurried out. Heard her booted feet following and waited for her on the rough-board walk.

She dragged a half-drunk man at her side who staggered wildly when she drew up to give Levi an insolent stare.

"Ma'am." He suddenly didn't know what to say, but he hadn't come here to run from challenges of any kind. "Sort of surprised to see a lady in the saloon." He was even more surprised she wore form-fitting, faded brown britches. He shifted his gaze upward, crashed into her gaze. Her eyes impaled him. Light brown, almost golden. Hard to look at. Impossible to pull away from.

She leaned back on her heels and hooked her thumbs through her belt loops. "Did you?"

"Did I what?"

"See a lady." She didn't wait for his reply. "I don't claim to be a lady. I do what suits me without regard for silly rules."

"I see." Though in truth he didn't. What rules did she consider silly? Her words had the same ringing tone Matthew's voice carried as he rode away from their grandparents' farm and straight into trouble. He perceived she was another rebel. This was confirmation of his calling to this town. This woman needed redemption for sure.

"Mr. Powers. . .or Preacher Powers, or whatever you've a hankering to be called. . .I got no objection to hearing a sermon now and then. Certainly no objection to you reading the scriptures to us, but don't be thinking you can make rules for everyone to follow. Might be some will gladly do so. But I won't be one of them." She grabbed the elbow of the swaying wide-eyed man she'd dragged from the saloon, paused to give his horse the once-over. "Yours?"

"Mine."

Something flickered through her eyes before she dragged her friend down the street.

"Glory, you sure are a sharp-tongued woman," the drunk muttered. "But I don't mind." He threw an arm across the woman's shoulders, almost upsetting them both.

Levi took a step forward, thinking to extricate her from the man.

The squeak of the swinging doors signaled another person's arrival. "I wouldn't interfere if I was you."

Levi ground to a halt, though it took a great deal of effort.

"That girl could chew up a man like you and spit him out without a thought."

"Like me?" He turned to face the speaker. A man like so many he'd seen—his face work-hardened and full of weary discouragement.

"Allow me to introduce myself. Claud Wagoner." They shook hands. "You really going to start Sunday services?"

"I am." And so much more. He'd made a bargain with God and intended to keep it. *God, You work on Matt, and I'll work for You out here.*

Claud shook his head. "You're lucky Bull Johnson is away. He owns this saloon and wouldn't take kindly to you disrupting his business. If ya know what I mean."

"I expect I do."

"Bull would not make a good enemy."

Levi snorted. "Never known of a good enemy." His gaze had shifted back down the street where the girl and the drunk turned the corner and disappeared from view. "What's her name?"

"Who?" The man followed the direction of Levi's stare. "Oh her. That's Glory Hamilton."

Glory. An unusual name for an unusual woman.

"Best you stay away from her. She's not the sort a preacher man should spend time with."

He had no intention of spending time with any woman

except for the sake of turning her feet to the right path, but he wondered why Claud should have such an opinion and asked.

"She is wild as the winter wind. Why, she's a horse trader."

This Glory just got more and more interesting. No, that wasn't the word he meant. It was only that he saw clearly she was part of the reason the Lord had directed him to this place.

Levi tipped the brim of his hat in a good-bye gesture and gathered up the reins of his horse. He didn't bother to swing into the saddle but led the horse down the street giving each building careful study.

A mercantile that appeared to be doing a brisk business, a freight office, likewise busy, a barber shop also offering baths. He considered the two bits it would cost and decided he would save his money and take a dip in some quiet place in the river. There was a lawyer office and a hardware store with an array of shovels, picks, and buckets displayed in the window. The sign to his left read HOTEL, but it was like no hotel he'd ever seen. A rough building. The two windows on the front were missing panes. The door hung crookedly. Flies buzzed around a bucket and even across the street he could smell the contents. A glance as he passed revealed rotting piles of garbage to the side of the building and he shuddered. He guessed the rooms would be no more appealing. And knowing the sort of person who would stay there rather than outdoors in the clean air, he knew it wasn't a place where a man could expect to wake up with his belongings still in his possession.

He thought of the business close to the ferry. Bonners Ferry Stopping House offering home-cooked meals. That place looked a lot more appealing as temporary quarters. He'd also noticed a small shop offering to shoe a horse.

He'd make his way back there first chance he got and ask to borrow the man's tools so he could do a little work on his mount's hooves.

He came to the end of the businesses with modest houses tucked behind them and continued on, passing scattered shacks farther along the road.

A hunched figure trudged toward him. A shriveled woman struggling under the weight of an armload of wood.

He trotted toward her and dismounted as he reached her side. "Ma'am. Let me help."

She resisted his offer to carry the wood. "It's mine. Leave me alone."

"I only want to help. Let me carry it for you."

Reluctantly she released it and gave him serious study up and down his length. "You new here?"

"Yes ma'am." He gave his name and lifted his hat. "Where to?"

She pointed to a shack that looked like it would leave in a good wind.

He shortened his stride to match her slow shuffle and wondered if each step hurt. She was bent forward forty degrees.

They reached the front of the hovel and she stopped. "Here's good enough. Just put it down. I'll take it the rest of the way."

"I'll take it to your kitchen."

The sound grating from her throat was neither disgust nor amusement yet somehow both. Then she shouldered open the door. It scratched against the rough wood floor.

He stepped inside to see four bare walls he could touch with his fingers without moving. It was nothing more than a primitive entryway. He stepped through the second doorway to a room not much larger. In it stood a stove made out of an old barrel. A rough piece of lumber nailed to the wall served as table, sawed-off logs provided seating. A battered wooden bucket and two old tin cans made up the rest of the items. "You live here?" He managed to keep the shock from his voice. Barely. The place was hardly big enough to shelter a horse in a bad storm. He could see light through the cracks between the boards forming the walls, and he suspected from the damp smell that the roof leaked.

"So long as no one objects."

He couldn't imagine why anyone would, but here was another being needing his help. Levi prayed for wisdom on how to deal with this without offending the woman. As he considered his options, he arranged the wood near the stove. Far as he could tell, the woman had no food. He didn't need to glance out the window to see if she had a garden. It was too early in the season for anything but a few greens. His job finished, he brushed his hands. "Ma'am, I'm here to preach the gospel. Would you like me to read from the Bible?"

She sat cross-legged on the floor.

He did the same, facing her.

"Name's Ina Kish—the widow Kish. I used to be a churchgoing woman. But there's no church here."

"I aim to change that."

"Don't know if there's many Christian people around here. I've seen no evidence of it."

He hadn't either but refrained from saying so. "Then I guess my work is cut out for me." He always carried a small New Testament in his vest pocket. He pulled it out and read several verses, noting the tears glistening in the woman's eyes. A few minutes later, after a prayer with her, he departed.

But he didn't head back to Bonners Ferry. He rode along the valley until he found and shot some prairie grouse. He dressed them and took them back to the widow Kish.

Tears again sprang to her eyes. "You are a godsend."

"Thank you."

"It is me should be thanking you."

He touched the brim of his hat as he backed away. Her words of thanks were affirmation for his task. Already he'd found two people to help—both women. One who welcomed his help. The other, he sensed, would not.

Where did the horse-trading Glory hang her hat? She looked like she could provide her own game probably better than many men. But he felt her rebellion like a canker sore under his tongue.

He would make it a priority to locate her and find a way to break through that rebellious spirit.

ॐ

Glory didn't slow her steps until she rounded the corner out of sight of the preacher. She wanted nothing to do with a cowboy intent on reforming others. No man would ever tell her what to do. No woman either, for that matter, unless it was one of her sisters.

She realized she held Toby by the elbow and practically dragged him after her, although half the time he dragged her to the right as he lost his balance.

"Glory, what's the hurry?" He struggled for breath. "Whatcha running from?"

She stopped and gave him a chance to right himself. "I never run from anything. You ought to know that."

Toby nodded. "You're pretty tough. Especially for a girl."

She let it pass.

He shifted his gaze to their back trail. "I thought I heard him say he was a preacher."

He didn't expect an answer, and Glory didn't provide one.

"Sure never seen a preacher like him before."

"That's a fact." She made a movement suggesting they should continue on their way, and Toby started again. Steady enough now to walk on his own. That meant she had found him before he got seriously drunk.

"Did you see his vest?"

Of course she'd seen his vest. Hand-tooled leather with Concho-style front leather ties and a fringed yoke. She'd seen a whole lot more. The thickness of his fawn-colored hair that couldn't be disguised or hidden by his hat. His square jaw that said better than words he meant business. The way his blue eyes slanted in hard assessment when he studied Glory. "I don't care what the man thinks."

"But his vest. No preacher wears a vest like that. Nor a hat like that either." Toby ground to a halt and struggled to retain his balance. "Say, I bet he ain't even a preacher. Seems I saw a poster once about a crook who wore a fancy vest. They call him the Rawhide Kid. I heard he pretends to be a nice guy then steals everything but the ground beneath your feet."

Rawhide Kid. Suited him better than preacher. Toby might have something in his rambling observations. What better disguise than posing as a preacher? It would fool a lot of people, especially when he read from the Bible in that deep ringing voice.

But she wasn't one to be fooled by well-spoken words or a rumbling voice that no doubt made others think of thunder rolling from heaven, the very voice of God even. Nope. Not Glory Hamilton. If she had learned one thing in her nineteen years it was to trust only what she could build and hold in her own two hands. Figuratively speaking.

She'd be keeping a close eye on the rawhide preacher. "Come on, Toby. You need to get some wood for Joanna."

"Aw."

"That's the agreement. Remember? You help Joanna around the stopping house in exchange for meals." Glory and her sisters, Joanna and Mandy, ran the stopping house.

Joanna was the cook. Mandy, the hunter. Glory. . .well, Glory did whatever was needed unless she could get Toby to do it.

"I can work for Bull, and he gives me cash."

"Which you promptly give back to him in the saloon. Good deal for Bull. Not such a good deal for you."

Toby muttered something about it feeling good right now.

Glory chose to ignore the comment. If Toby didn't do the agreed-upon work, Joanna would be after Glory to do it, and Glory had other things to do with her time. She managed to steer Toby to the stopping house and turned him over to Joanna who issued instructions to get firewood and water, take out ashes, and empty the slop pail.

Toby explained to Joanna about the man in the saloon. "Said he was a preacher."

"Bonners Ferry could use a preacher and a church, too," Joanna said, slanting a pointed look at Glory.

"He can preach his heart out. Won't change me."

Joanna sighed. "You're always so defensive. No one said anything about changing you. But comes a time in all of our lives when we have to stop running from life and simply learn to trust God with it."

"I trust God."

"Trusting covers a lot of things."

"I hate it when you get all philosophical. You got something to say, come right out and say it."

Joanna handed the bucket of vegetable peelings to Toby and waved him away. "All I'm saying is. . ." She shrugged. "I don't know. Never mind. I suppose I mean for myself more than anyone else. Where are you off to?"

Glory laughed. "Who said I am."

Joanna lifted one eyebrow in mocking amusement. "Let's see. Could it be because you keep shifting from one foot to the other and glancing toward the door? Or maybe because

I know you well enough I just know?"

"Probably both. I want to check on those horses I have up the hill."

"You'll be back for supper?"

"Of course. And I'll wash the dishes and sweep the floor and whatever else needs doing."

"Good. Then go see to your horses."

Glory reached for the door.

"Glory."

Her sister's voice stopped her.

"Be careful. Some of those horses you rescue are mean."

"They have reason to be." She too often saw horses neglected and abused. When she did, she tried to buy them from the owners and nurse them back to health, train them to be good mounts, and sell them to men who would treat them right. She'd keep them all if she could, but it wasn't practical, and selling them provided her with funds to buy more to help.

"I'm not saying they don't. But you are up there alone. I worry."

"No need. I never take chances. You know that."

Another quirk of Joanna's telltale eyebrow. "I certainly do."

Glory shook her head in bewilderment. Joanna seemed set on talking in riddles or raising questions she didn't intend to answer. And Glory had no time for such nonsense. She left the stopping house, crossed to the shop where she ran a small farrier business and kept her current mount.

The beautiful palomino was nothing but a bag of bones when she rescued him. The gelding now glistened with health and had turned out to be a smooth ride. It was one of the times she thought seriously of keeping an animal. Indeed, unless she was offered a good price, she wouldn't let him go.

She threw on a saddle and swung to the animal's back.

"Come on, Pal. Let's go visit your friends."

In order to reach the place, she had to ride back through town. Past the saloon where the rawhide preacher had hitched his black horse. A beautiful horse. But the horse no longer waited patiently. The pair must have moved on. She tried to put them from her mind. But instead, the piercing gaze of the man seemed to glaze her thoughts to the exclusion of all else.

Rawhide Kid.

A desperado. A criminal. A confidence man.

Not above using the Bible as a means of portraying the picture he wanted to create.

Yet...

She jerked her thoughts away from how he'd boldly walked into the saloon and opened the Holy Word. *'Course if Bull had been there he might have gone out on his ear.*

As if her thoughts didn't have enough trouble erasing him, she glimpsed a big black horse in the woods. Had to be the rawhide preacher man. What subversive thing was he up to? Perhaps he had partners in crime hiding, awaiting the chance to steal from the good citizens of Bonners Ferry.

She pulled her own horse off the path and dismounted, hiding as best she could behind a patch of trees to watch.

In a minute, he broke from the trees and sauntered up the trail.

She let him pass, then, keeping to the leaf-protected ground at the edge of the trail, followed at a safe distance behind him.

He turned in at the shack where Widow Kish lived, swung off the horse without touching the saddle horn, and landed neatly on his feet. He reached behind him and lifted off two dressed birds and carried them inside.

She squatted in the dappled shadows and waited. If he had harmed the widow and taken possession of her shack. . .well, he would have to answer to her. The smell of wood smoke drew her attention to the battered piece of stovepipe poking through the roof. Smoke billowed upward. She waited.

Then the door sqawked open and he stepped out into the sun. Bareheaded, his hat in his hand, the sun glistening in his hair.

"I can't thank you enough." The widow patted his hand.

"My pleasure." He jammed his hat on, swung into the saddle in one swift movement, and reined toward town.

Glory remained where she was, watching until he rode down the hill and out of sight. Still she didn't move. What was he doing? Was he playing some kind of game intended to make everyone trust him?

He'd soon learn Glory Hamilton didn't trust so easily.

She pushed to her feet, pulled Pal back to the path, and got on his back with a lot less grace and ease than the preacher did. The fact did nothing to ease her suspicions.

A few minutes later she arrived at the temporary corrals she'd built for her horses, and her mood immediately improved. Animals were so uncomplicated. Treat them right and they rewarded with loyalty. Most wanted to please, and those that didn't learned the joys of obeying given enough patience and kindness. She knew how to give plenty of both.

One big gray gelding snorted and reared away as soon as she approached. He would take a long time to realize she meant him no harm. But at least his wounds had healed nicely.

"Don't worry, big guy. I'm not going to rush you." She threw handfuls of oats from her saddlebag to each of the horses. Big Gray wouldn't go near his treat until she backed away, but every day she gained ground. "Won't be long until you're eating out of my hand." He didn't snort and act up at her voice anymore.

She spent the better part of the afternoon with the animals.

This place was perfect. Close enough to town she could tend the horses each day. High enough to not suffer from the spring floods. There were lots of trees, a stream that ran throughout the summer, open sunny patches of grass, and a view that filled her with pleasure. Too bad she didn't own it. But no one had objected to her using it, and until someone did. . . She hoped when the time came she would be able to buy this bit of land.

It was time to leave unless she wanted Joanna to send some young buck in search of her. Joanna had done it before. She'd do it again. She took her role as eldest sister seriously.

Glory caught up to Pal, threw the saddle on again, and rode back to the stopping house. Basins of water and towels were set out in the lean-to entryway, and Glory stopped to wash off the smell of horse as best she could.

A rumble of voices came from the long dining room. Sounded like a full house. They usually served about twenty travelers and a handful of regulars. Which meant lots of dishes to wash. There'd be no getting out of it today. She'd already promised Joanna. Besides, it was the least Glory could do. Joanna did the bulk of the work, never complaining. Mandy spent long hours out in the woods keeping the place supplied with fresh meat. Glory had to contribute in some way, even if it was drudge work like washing dishes and cleaning floors.

She dried her hands and swiped them over her hair making sure it was relatively free of grass then stepped into the noisy room, giving a quick glance around to see who was in attendance. Her gaze skidded to a halt at the man sitting at the far corner of the table. Levi Powers.

His eyes met hers across the distance, and at the way they narrowed, she knew he was as surprised to see her as she was to see him. And she felt a silent challenge as his gaze swept over her dungarees and back to her face, checking her hair.

She clenched her fists at her sides to keep from brushing her hands over her hair again. Nothing he did would make her ashamed or embarassed about who she was and how she chose to dress. Nothing he did or said would make her change.

Nothing.

She spun away and marched into the kitchen, her boots ringing with more force than normal. She grabbed two heaping bowls from the service table. "What's he doing here?" Her voice was harsh, accusing, as if it was Joanna's fault.

Joanna chuckled. "You'll have to be more specific. At my count there are twenty-one men in there."

"The preacher. Why is he here?"

Joanna lifted one shoulder dismissively. "Because he paid me to eat here. Isn't that what we do? Feed people who pay?"

Glory choked back her protest. Yes, it was what they did. The few dollars that were her share of the profit filled a tin can. Slowly. Someday it would be enough to buy her precious piece of land. "Of course it's what we do."

She carried the bowls into the dining room, put them down, and chose a spot on the long bench at the far corner of the room from Mr. Powers. She spared him the briefest glare. Let him think what he wanted of her. If he even thought of her.

Joanna took her place at the end of the table, close to Powers. Mandy found room on a crowded bench next to Toby. Joanna signaled quiet. "We are a Christian family and always say a blessing before the meal."

Glory allowed herself a flicker of her eyes toward Powers and was pleased to see his surprise. *Just goes to show you can't judge people,* she silently crowed.

Joanna continued. "Today we have a special guest at the table. Mr. Powers. Preacher Powers. He's going to start services here in Bonners Ferry. Now I know most of you won't be here past the night, but for those of you who are, I'm sure you're as happy as I that we're going to have a church."

Glory kept her gaze glued to the tin plate in front of her. She wasn't pleased at all. Besides, who—other than himself—said he was a preacher? Rawhide Kid for all they knew.

Joanna was still speaking. "Mr. Powers, we'd be pleased if you'd ask the blessing tonight." She lifted a hand toward him in invitation.

Powers pushed to his feet and looked at each one around the table.

Glory refused to meet his glance. She demanded a whole lot more than his say-so to believe he was a preacher and nothing more, nothing less.

two

Levi struggled to his feet. The heavy bench, held in place by so many bodies, pressed against his calves. He half-welcomed the discomfort, nailing him to reality as it did.

He'd been some surprised to learn the Bonners Ferry Stopping House was run by three sisters. But the smell of supper convinced him to stay. He'd met Miss Joanna when he paid for his meal, noted she wore a split skirt under her big white apron. He'd met Miss Mandy as she skittered away when he went to wash up. Miss Mandy carried a dozen prairie grouse and hung them on a nail. She wore baggy pants and a big slouch hat. So he shouldn't have been surprised when Miss Glory slid to an empty spot at the table.

Except he was. Somehow he thought she'd be hunkered down by a campfire someplace deep in the woods. Exactly why he thought such a thing baffled him. Sure, she looked a little rough around the edges, and her gaze, as she glared at him, suggested she didn't much care what people thought. Him in particular. But just the same, his assumptions were foolish. Of course she had family. Likely friends. The young man she'd dragged from the saloon sat further along the bench. Finding her in a saloon, befriending a man who had been partaking, he supposed his mistaken idea came from evidence she herself had provided.

He shepherded his thoughts back to his purpose. "Folks, I'm here to bring God's Word into this area. I'm available if you want to hear it read, or talk about His love, or pray. Feel free to come to me at any time. I'm looking for a suitable

21

place to hold Sunday services. I expect we'll meet outdoors for a few weeks. Now let us pray." He bowed his head and asked God's blessing on the food, thanking God for His many mercies.

For several minutes after he sat down, the food was passed, plates loaded, and people put their attention to eating before they began talking. Much of the conversation centered on the trail ahead. Most of those present were headed for the Kootenais to look for gold. Hope and desperation hung like flags over the table.

Levi listened to the man on his right tell how he'd sold everything and left his wife and children with her parents. "I aim to make enough to buy myself a piece of land and build a big house."

"And if you don't?" It always bothered him that pursuing dreams without considering reality so often led to desperate actions.

The man shuddered. "I don't think I could continue to face life."

Levi had let his gaze and attention wander to Glory who was in animated conversation with the man next to her. What had her so enthused? But his attention returned to the man at his side, and he dismissed all other distractions in his concern for the confession from the man's lips. "If you find yourself in such a situation, I urge you to pray and ask God to provide direction to something productive. There are always alternatives to desperation." Just as there were always alternatives to crime, though he didn't voice the thought.

Suddenly everyone pushed back as if given a signal. He hadn't been watching. Perhaps Miss Joanna had indicated the meal was over.

She spoke now. "For those planning to spend the night, the room will be ready by eight. Feel free to return then and claim a spot. In the meantime, you are welcome to make yourself comfortable outside and enjoy the sunshine."

Levi had noticed benches outside against the walls of the stopping house and guessed she meant those.

Joanna continued. "Ladies"—she referred to the four female guests—"you're welcome to stay indoors if you prefer."

Mandy strode outside, lifted the birds from the nail where she'd left them, and disappeared behind a shed in the far corner. Levi suspected she meant to dress them ready to cook.

He barely got his feet under him when Glory started to gather up the tin plates with a good deal of racket. She carried them into the kitchen and dropped them into a basin of water.

He made his way to the door.

A great amount of clattering came from the kitchen.

He emerged into the slanted evening sun and leaned against the warm wall.

The young man he'd seen with Glory sidled up to him. "Hi, I'm Toby."

He shook hands with the younger man.

"You really a preacher?"

"I am."

"Where all you preached?"

"Several places." He named two towns in the Dakotas where he'd done what he could and moved on, ever wanting to do more.

"So whatcha doing here? This here is a tight ship, as my pa would say."

Levi didn't know if he meant the town or the stopping house and didn't care to discuss it. He had his work cut out for him whether a kid who got drunk in the middle of the afternoon thought so or not. "Where's your pa?" Seemed

Toby ought to be with a parent still.

"Back home in Indiana."

From the open door came more clattering. Washing tin plates seemed to be a noisy affair.

Joanna, working in the dining room, called out, "Glory, could you keep the noise down a mite? My ears are hurting."

Levi grinned deep inside. Seems something was annoying Miss Glory to the point of taking it out on innocent dishes. Could be one of the reasons the stopping house used tin plates.

Toby leaned back against the wall, shoulder to shoulder with Levi, by all looks, intent on a long chin wag. Well, it was what Levi had invited. Part of what he'd vowed to do. The words he'd said to God on his knees guided his every decision. *Lord, You work on Matt where he is, and I'll work for You out here.*

"I was headed for the Kootenai gold fields. Sort of ran out of steam about here."

Levi read between the lines. Ran out of money. Ran into a saloon.

"The buffalo gals sort of helped me out, if you know what I mean."

Levi did. "Buffalo gals?"

Toby tipped his head toward the door. "That's what they call them three."

"How so?"

Toby shrugged. "Can't say. Never asked anyone. It just is."

It just is. Seems a lot of life was like that. No reason for why things were. No reason for parents dying and leaving two boys orphaned. No reason for one choosing to follow God, the other choosing to run wild. Except—Levi's teeth clenched of their own accord—he believed things could be different. If someone would show kindness to the hurting, reach out a hand to those in need. . .

It was what his task was. He'd do it to the best of his ability and trust God to do His share where Levi couldn't.

Another man, dressed in a suit better fitted for sitting behind a desk, edged toward Levi. He waited for a break in the conversation. "Can I talk to you?"

"Certainly."

"It's kind of private."

"Of course." He unwound himself from the wall and followed the man away from the crowd toward a place where they appeared to be alone.

The man looked around to be sure before he spoke. "Preacher, would you pray for me?"

"By all means. What shall I pray?" He listened to the man's story, read some encouraging scriptures, and prayed.

By then the sun was setting, sending flares of red, orange, and pink across the Kootenai River. He'd planned to set up camp in a quiet spot among the trees, but now it was too late to find a decent spot. And it seemed he could best live up to his purpose if he stayed closer to town and hung around the stopping house, which practically burst with people.

Besides, if he stayed, perhaps he could talk to Glory and find out what made her eyes glint like sun off a rifle barrel every time he glanced at her. Seemed the gal had a mighty big grudge fueling her audaciousness.

Levi had left his saddle and bedroll in the lean-to, which served as luggage area for all those at the stopping house. He gathered up his bedding and headed inside. He dropped the necessary coins in Joanna's palm and looked about the dining room. The table had been pushed against the wall, the benches tucked underneath, leaving plenty of floor space. The ladies had disappeared into the far room where two big beds allowed them a measure of comfort and privacy.

"Help yourself." Joanna waved about the room. Where had the other two Hamilton girls disappeared to?

Already several places had been claimed by way of unrolled bedding and sometimes a carpetbag. He chose a spot close to the kitchen door with his back to the wall and sank to the floor. He opened his Bible and began to read. That's when he heard voices from the kitchen and recognized Miss Glory and Miss Mandy.

"I still think we should be trying to find Pa." He knew immediately it was Miss Mandy whose voice was softer, gentler than Glory's.

"Don't see why. We got a nice situation here."

"He's our pa."

"I know. And how many times have we caught up to him, think we're part of his life, when he up and disappears?"

"Glory, he's just trying to make a living."

"Mandy, you can dream things are the way you wish they were, but they aren't. Truth is, Pa is restless. More concerned with scratching his restless itch than worrying about three daughters. Besides, aren't we big enough to take care of ourselves now?"

Levi listened shamelessly, hearing the harshness in Glory's voice but hearing so much more beneath—a history of pain.

Glory reminded him so strongly of Matt whose disappointment and frustration had led to his recklessness. If someone had reached out to Matt before it was too late. . .

Thank You, God, for this glimpse, this insight into what makes her tick.

Suddenly Glory stood in the doorway. "You're staying here?"

"Paid my money to your sister." He knew that wasn't what she meant. She simply objected to his presence, but he wouldn't give her the satisfaction of acknowledging it.

She made a protesting noise deep in her throat but didn't voice her disapproval in words. Perhaps because Joanna watched them. Instead she marched toward the door. "I'm going to check on Pal."

"It's late. Almost dark," Joanna protested.

"I'll go with her," Mandy said.

Glory stopped and planted her hands on her hips, glaring from one sister to the other. "I do not need a nanny. Or a mother. Or a guard. Or. . .or. . ."

Joanna waved her away. "I expect the two of you back soon so I can close the doors."

Exasperation burst from Glory's mouth in an explosive sound, and she tossed her hands in the air in a gesture Levi took as defeat.

He grinned.

She slanted him a glare with the power to straighten his mouth and make him sit up straighter. "I need no one and nothing," she muttered before she strode out the door.

Levi's grin returned as soon as the door closed behind her.

Joanna stepped past him into the kitchen area and settled at the table, entering figures into a big ledger and likely waiting for her younger sisters to return. She left the door between open partway so she could keep an eye on the outer door for more overnight guests.

Many of the men had tucked into their bedrolls already. Several snored loudly.

But Levi sat up, continuing to read by the faint lantern light from the kitchen. He wouldn't settle down until he knew Glory and her sisters were safely in their beds.

❧

Glory steamed after Mandy, hot air burning from her lungs. Why had that man chosen to spend the night at the stopping house? Seems a real preacher would have found a quiet place to sleep.

Like a hundred miles away straight up the tallest mountain.

They reached Glory's shop, and she made a great show of filling Pal's water trough, checking the gate, and examining the inside of her shop. As if someone might have moved in and taken over.

Just like Levi had taken over every spare thought in her head. Oh, how she hated that she couldn't stop thinking of him. "I think I'll go check on the other horses." They didn't need it any more than Pal did, but returning to the stopping house, knowing that man was there made her skin feel too small.

"You can't do that. It's nearly dark already."

"I can do it if I want." She sounded petty and childish but couldn't seem to help it.

"Why are you so angry? It's because of Mr. Powers, isn't it? I saw the way you kept looking at him."

She ignored her sister's questions. They didn't deserve acknowledgment.

"Why does he bother you? He's here to start a church. Seems you should be glad for such a thing."

Glory snorted. "Who says he's a preacher? Besides him. And why should we believe him? He could say he was anything, and we'd have no way of knowing. Does he have papers to prove it?"

"Glory, listen to yourself. We didn't ask Mr. Murray to prove he was a lawyer. No one asked us for proof we could run a stopping house."

"Proof is in the product, I'd say. We run a good clean establishment with satisfying meals and rules about conduct."

"Then I guess Mr. Powers deserves the same consideration. A chance to prove himself."

Glory stared at her sister. Should she tell her of the suspicions? Mention that Toby thought Powers looked like a robber on a wanted poster? "Did you see his vest?"

Mandy grinned. "Sure did. You think he'd sell it?"

Glory rolled her eyes. "Who cares?"

Mandy got a faraway look on her face. "I suppose you noticed how handsome he is."

"Is not."

Mandy's gaze jerked to Glory, disbelief written in every line. "Is too."

Not prepared to argue with her younger sister, Glory simply rolled her head back and forth.

Mandy suddenly crowed and slapped her thighs. "You think he's too good-looking to be a preacher."

Glory favored her sister with a scalding look but utterly failed to curb Mandy's amusement. Finally, unable to stand still for the mockery, she placed a playful punch on Mandy's shoulder.

Mandy immediately turned and cuffed Glory on the side of the head.

This was a familiar game they played, throwing pretend punches, dancing back and forth in mock attack. As usual they ended locked in each other's arms, squirming and laughing.

"I give," Glory called.

It didn't matter who said it first. It was all in fun. They broke apart, grinning at each other.

"Give the man a chance, even if he is too handsome for his own good," Mandy said, throwing her arm across Glory's shoulders as they headed for home.

"Best I can do is try and stay away from him." Though she intended to watch him carefully and wondered how she could do both at the same time.

They quieted as they reached the stopping house, knowing some of their guests would already be asleep, and tiptoed inside to the kitchen.

Joanna sat at the table and closed the ledger as they entered. The three headed toward their quarters beyond—a small bedroom on the far side of the kitchen from the room where their guests slept. Glory brought up the rear, and as they crossed the floor, Levi murmured, "Good night. Sleep well."

Glory broke her stride, struggled to control her annoyance. Then sucked in air and hurried along. How was she to ignore him if he wouldn't let her?

three

Levi left after breakfast—a meal eaten in haste as if people were anxious to be on their way.

Glory had pointedly ignored him all through the meal then hurried to the kitchen and disappeared.

What did it matter? He planned to be around a long time. . . or at least as long as it took to accomplish his purpose.

He rode over to the shop to see about trimming Billy Bob's hooves. A sign tacked to the door said, OPEN 9 TO NOON. COME BACK THEN. That would be another hour. Time enough to check on the widow Kish.

He detoured into the mercantile and purchased a few supplies then stopped at the hardware store for a new bucket, which he filled at the town pump and carried carefully to the shack on the edge of town. At the door, he saw a basket covered with a bit of rag and folded it back to see four eggs, a loaf of bread, and six potatoes. He covered the basket again and grinned up at the sky, silently thanking God someone else cared about the widow's dire circumstances. Somehow it made him feel he shared the task with a person of like mind.

His knock brought the widow shuffling to the door. He tipped his head to indicate the basket, and she scooped it up and peeked under the cover.

"The Lord provides," she murmured. "Blessed be His name. About once a week I find a basket like this on the step. And now you bring me water from the well. The good Lord says a cup of cold water given in His name is rewarded. I'm sure you'll receive an even greater reward for a whole bucketful."

"It's nice to see you feeling better. Yesterday you looked about ready to lie down and die."

"That's about how I felt, but my faith is renewed."

He spent a few minutes with her. "I'll be back tomorrow." He left feeling she had given him far more than he gave her.

She waved him away. "If you're so all-fired set on helping people, why don't you check on Mr. Phelps? I've not seen him for several days." She led him to the door and pointed out a modest house several yards down the trail toward town.

"I'll do that." He rode to the house, dismounted, and hung the reins over the hitching post. His boots echoed on the wooden steps as he approached the entrance. His knock rattled the door and rang through the house.

No one answered.

He knocked again and called out, "Mr. Phelps? Are you in there?" Still no sound apart from his own voice. He tried the door. It opened and swung inward. The place had a sour, sick smell to it. "Mr. Phelps? Is anyone here?" Did he hear a faint sound through the door to his left? "I'm coming in."

He stepped into a kitchen. A half-eaten meal remained on the table, but the stove was cold, the room slightly dampish from being unheated. If he had to guess, he'd say it had been more than a day or two since the stove had been lit.

A door stood past the stove, and he crossed to it and pushed it open. The sour smell practically knocked him back on his heels. An untidy soiled cot stood in one corner, the covers tossed to the floor in disarray. A wardrobe, a chiffonier, and a wooden rocker completed the furnishings. He half-turned away when he noticed the pile of blankets on the floor move. Someone or something was in that mess. He crossed the room in two strides and eased the fabric aside.

A man lay there, as white as death, soiled from head to bottom.

"Mr. Phelps, I assume?"

The man flickered a look of acknowledgment.

"You've been sick." Levi wondered how long the poor man had lain in his own filth. He threw aside the soiled blankets, scooped the man into his arms, and gently laid him on the cot. "You're safe now." He found a clean blanket and covered the man. "I'll clean you up and take care of you."

First thing Mr. Phelps needed was water. Levi hoofed it back to the kitchen, found two empty buckets, and dashed outside to see if the man had a well. He hated the idea of leaving the man to go into town for water, though it wasn't far. But he'd need lots of it.

He looked about, saw no pump, and wished for an alternative to trotting back to town. *God, perhaps You could send help.* He heard the clop of a horse and raced around the house, back to the trail.

Glory headed toward him on a beautiful palamino horse. He'd seen the horse yesterday, standing contentedly in a small pen next to the farrier's shop.

He waved and called.

She reined in. "What are you doing in the middle of the road yelling like a mad man?"

"I only—" He didn't have time to argue though he wanted badly to say he only called out for her to stop. "I need help with Mr. Phelps."

"What's wrong? Is he hurt?" Her expression shifted so suddenly it startled him.

"He's ill. I need water and lots of it, but I don't see a pump on his place."

"No, he gets water from the town supply."

"Do you think—?" He held the buckets toward her.

She yanked them from his hands, almost taking his arms off at the shoulders. "Be right back." And she kicked the horse into a run.

Levi stared after her. Talk about mercurial. But he didn't have time to worry about how Glory chose to act. Mr. Phelps needed attention.

Levi found a wood supply, carried an armload to the house, and built a fire. They'd need a barrel of hot water to clean Mr. Phelps and his bedding.

He explained to the man he would have water in a few minutes then gathered up the soiled laundry and hauled it outside. He located a washtub hanging on the side of the house and dumped the bedding into it. As soon as he had water, he would put it to soak.

While he was out, Glory returned. By the time he got to the house, she had filled a pitcher with water, dumped some in the reservoir to heat, and headed back for more water.

Levi shook his head. The woman was as unpredictable as the weather.

He took a glass of water to Mr. Phelps then filled a kettle and set it to boil. He was in the bedroom, sponging Mr. Phelps, when Glory returned, her boots ringing across the floor as she carried water to the reservoir and filled it. "Miss Glory," he called, but she was gone. She returned twice more while Levi cared for Mr. Phelps, found clean bedding and a clean nightshirt, and made the man comfortable.

"Powers," Glory called from the kitchen.

Levi went to the door.

"There's water soaking the bedding. I filled every container in the house. What else do you need?"

Levi stared at her. Water soaked her britches to the knees, and her hat hung down her back as if she had ridden furiously back and forth. Sometimes her wild behavior had a bonus to it. She'd brought more water in less time than any other woman, and many a man, could have done.

"Powers?"

He shook himself back to the task at hand. "The man is weak. He needs something gentle to eat. Don't suppose you know where I could get some chicken soup for him?"

She spared him a look rife with disbelief. "I don't know of anyone with chickens to butcher, and no one around here would kill a laying hen." Then she brightened. "But Joanna had venison stewing on the stove. That'll do." And she was gone so fast Levi could do nothing but stare after her.

One more task to be done. There was no avoiding it. He removed his vest and hung it over the back of a chair, rolled up his sleeves, and went outside to take care of the laundry.

He heard Glory return, but he was up to his elbows in hot sudsy water.

She poked her head out the door, saw what he was doing, and grimaced. "I'll see if Mr. Phelps will take some broth." She closed the door firmly after her.

Levi laughed aloud. "Trade you," he called.

Her muffled voice came from the other side of the door. "Not this time."

He laughed again. She might be wild as an unbroken horse, rebellious and headed for trouble like his brother, but he certainly appreciated her help.

He rinsed the sheets and strung them over the clothesline, dumped out the water, and returned the tub to the nail where he'd found it. As he headed back inside, he heard Glory ride away and stopped to stare out the window, wondering why she hadn't stayed. Was she that anxious to avoid contact with him? Never mind. They would spend time together somehow, somewhere. He'd see to it.

After he checked again on Mr. Phelps, promising to return later in the day, he returned to Widow Kish and reported on her neighbor.

"I'll maybe go on over and check on him myself. Poor man."

Levi thought it might do her a world of good to have something to do. Time now to return to town and attend to Billy Bob's hooves.

Glory's palimino was in the pen again. Must be where she kept her horse. The door to the shop was open, and he stepped inside.

Glory looked up from a book she read. "Yes?" When she saw it was him, her welcome faded. She seemed to struggle a moment with her reaction and schooled it away. "Mr. Phelps okay now?"

"He was resting. Widow Kish said she'd go check on him. Thanks for your help this morning."

"He's one of us, and you're a stranger. Why wouldn't I help him?"

Words of protest raced to his tongue, but he bit them back. Soon enough she'd see he meant to be one of them, too.

"What can I do for you?" Right words, begrudgingly spoken.

"My horse needs his hooves trimmed."

"Great. Put him in the corral, and I'll tend to it."

"Uh." She was a farrier? Not that it surprised him all that much. He had about figured out Glory could do anything she set her mind to, no matter how unconventional. "I was hoping you'd lend me the tools so I can do it myself."

She shook her head. "Don't lend my tools." She stuck a rasp in her back pocket, lifted the nippers in one hand and the hoof knife in the other, and headed for the side door opening to the pen. "Bring him here, and I'll do it."

" 'Fraid not. You see, my horse is particular about who gets close to him."

She strode past him to stand looking at Billy Bob. "Nice-looking horse."

"Yup. Many have admired him. Few have ridden him."

She turned, her eyes flaring with interest. "How's that?"

"He's a one-man horse."

Her gaze shifted from Levi to the horse then back to Levi. "Really?" Her voice rang with doubt.

"Take my word for it."

She reached out for Billy Bob's reins and headed for the gate. "He's coming along fine." She closed the gate after the horse and put her tools on a stump obviously used for that purpose. "Now let's get at this job."

"Glory, listen to me." He rushed forward and took the reins before she could do anything more. "He won't let you touch him."

"I never met a horse I couldn't handle." She positioned herself in front of Billy Bob.

Knowing what would happen, Levi pushed the horse away.

Glory turned and glared at him. "Let me do my job."

"Lend me your tools, and I'll do it. If it's the money you're worried about, I'll pay the same as if you did it."

Her chin jutted out. "I don't lend my tools. Now hold his head so I can look at his foot." She again stood, her back to Billy Bob, and leaned over to touch his leg.

Levi moved as fast as he could, but Billy Bob was faster and got a chunk of Glory's rump between his teeth.

Glory yelped and jumped away.

Levi pulled at Billy Bob's head. "Stop it, you blockhead." He kept a firm hold on the animal as he glanced over his shoulder at Glory. "Are you okay?"

The surprise in her face shifted to defiance. "I'm fine. Why didn't you tell me he bites?"

"Glory Hamilton, you have got to be the most cantankerous woman alive. I warned you he wouldn't let you touch him. But you wouldn't listen. Now all of a sudden it's my fault? Just stay away from my horse and give me the hoof pick."

Still she hesitated. All kinds of names came to mind. Foolish. Ornery. Stubborn. Headstrong. "I'll pay. Just let me deal with this."

Reluctantly she handed him the pick.

He bent over and took a hoof and set to cleaning it.

"I see lots of horses who have bad attitudes. Usually there's a reason. What's the story behind Billy Bob's behavior?"

"Bought him off a farmer a few years ago. He was in pretty bad shape. The farmer shouldn't have been allowed to have animals the way he treated them. Hand me the nippers, would you?"

She seemed reluctant to put the tools where he could reach them himself but at least handed him what he needed without further argument, for which he was grateful.

"I tended his wounds and gave him lots of good feed. In return he is as loyal as one could ever ask. Just won't let anyone else touch him. The rasp please."

She handed it to him and took the nippers in exchange.

Seemed she meant to hang about and watch his every move. He meant to take advantage of it. "Where's your pa?"

"Guess you heard my ma is dead. My pa is off looking for gold in the Kootenais."

He had Billy Bob stand so he could check the hoof was level then took up the next foot. "Why do they call you the Buffalo Gals?"

"Why do you ask? You planning to write a book or something?"

"Don't get all prickly. I'm just making polite conversation."

"No. Polite conversation is, 'How are you? Nice weather we're having, don't you think? Did you enjoy the sunshine yesterday? Suppose we might get rain?'"

He laughed, earning him a scowl. "Do you?"

"Do I what?"

He straightened and grinned at her, undeterred by her annoyance. "Suppose we might get rain?"

She lifted her hands in mock frustration. "Mud just dried up from the spring runoff. I would like to enjoy a few days mud free."

"What about the sunshine? You enjoy it yesterday?"

A smile lifted the corners of her mouth. "Sure did."

Curiosity about how she spent her days crowded all else from his mind. "What did you do?"

"Let's see. I had a race with two men off the ferry who thought they could ride better'n a girl. I proved them wrong." She laughed. "I took care of three horses a man had neglected to trim hooves on for some time." A teasing light flashed across her eyes. "And of course, I spent time in the saloon."

He knew a challenging tone and expression when he saw it. For a moment they did silent battle with their eyes. He decided to let it pass. After all, he had lots of time to find what drove her to defy all sense of what was right as if she resented being a woman. "So why do they call you the Buffalo Gals?"

She blinked, and he knew she'd been expecting him to say something about her being in the saloon. "Because of Pa." She scowled as if she'd said more than she meant to. "Pa was a buffalo hunter, among other things." Before he could ask what other things, she guessed his question and provided an answer. "Gold prospector, Indian hunter, guide, railroad worker—" She drew in a deep breath. "There isn't much he hasn't tried."

He heard a "but" in her voice and waited, but she seemed inclined to say no more and fiddled with the nail nippers. Levi turned his attention back to Billy Bob's feet, but his mind twirled her words about, trying to find the "but" in them. "Sounds like he's a wanderer."

"Suppose so."

"He take you girls with him?"

"When Ma was alive, she followed him, and after she died, we just continued to follow him like she'd taught us."

Again he mulled over her words, looking for the meaning beneath them. "When did your ma die?"

"Eight years ago, when I was eleven."

He put Billy Bob's foot down, done with the hoof trimming, and studied Glory. She stared off into the distance, and Levi wondered if she even remembered he was there. Was this the pain she tried to kill with her outrageous behavior?

He shifted his gaze to the end of her shop, saw a For Rent sign. Saw the flicker of red gingham at a window next to the sign, caught a glimpse of a table and stove. Let his gaze go further, to the blue sky, the distant purple mountains.

But what he saw was inside his heart. The way Matt had run from the pain of their parents' deaths. His refusal to follow any rules—those laid out by their grandparents who took them in and gave them a home or those made by man. And look where it had led him.

Levi felt the same angry desperation in Glory as if she, like Matt, didn't know how to deal with the way life had turned out. He feared her path would take her perilously close to the same destination it had for Matt—a prison sentence. *God, I'm here to do Your work in Bonners Ferry, and I trust You to do Your work in Matt's prison cell.* "Glory, you can't fix your disappointment in life by defying all the rules."

Her gaze hit him with the blast of a blacksmith's fire. "Who appointed you judge and jury of me? Besides, I am not disappointed with life." Her laugh was bitter. "Shows what you know." She spun on her heels. "Pal, come." The horse trotted over to her. She swung up on his bare back and guided him toward the gate where she leaned over to unhook it and throw it open. "Put the tools away. Leave your money on the table." And she kicked her horse into a gallop, clinging to his back without saddle or bridle, like some kind of wild Indian.

Levi stared after her, his throat tight. It was dangerous to ride in such a fashion. But he understood she cared nothing for the dangers involved. Whether or not she knew it, she was trying to outrun some kind of pain. But he'd pushed too hard, too soon, and now he'd lost ground that would take precious time to regain.

≥∂

Glory didn't allow Pal to slacken his pace until they reached the spot where her other horses munched on grass.

Three of them whinnied at her approach and ran toward the fence to greet her. Big Gray headed for the far side of the pen. The other two only lifted their heads to watch her.

She'd left in such a huff she'd neglected to bring oats for them. "I'll bring your treat next time, for sure." She enjoyed talking to all of the horses and giving them attention. Big Gray wouldn't let her near without oats.

She sank down in the warm grass and leaned her back to a tree. Powers was so annoying. Unsettling. She'd been surprised twice by his willingness to help those in need. Of course, what better way to give people the impression he was a preacher. But shouldn't he preach, maybe try and close down the saloon, instead of rolling up his sleeves and washing laundry?

She allowed herself a grin at the thought of his laboring over the washtub. For a moment, she'd almost liked him. Or at least, respected him. And then he got all. . .all. . . Well shoot, she didn't even know how to describe it. Preachy. Judgmental. And none of his business in the first place. Or the last.

She would do what she wanted so long as she broke no laws. And not because, as he seemed to think, she was disappointed with life. She loved life. She raised her arms to the sky and whooped. Life was good. Made for enjoyment. And she intended to enjoy it as never before.

Joanna had once taken them all to a circus with coins handed to her by their pa. They'd watched a man in tights do trick riding. It looked like so much fun. Joanna had noted her excitement, and the moment Glory opened her mouth to say she was going to do that, Joanna had grabbed her by the arm. "Pa holds me responsible for you and Mandy. If either of you gets hurt, it will be on my head. Promise you won't try such foolishness."

At first Glory had refused and tried to squirm away, but Joanna had a grip like a vise and wouldn't let her go until she promised.

But that was when Glory was a child. Joanna was no longer responsible for Glory. She answered to no one but herself and God.

She'd learned several of the riding tricks. Pal had turned out to be such a trustworthy mount, she had a great deal of fun standing on his back while they raced down the trail. It always made her heart beat fast. It was exhilarating. She had done the death drag several times. At first, it frightened her to see the ground so close to her head as she hung from the saddle by one leg, but conquering her fear, gaining confidence, was worth every risk.

An idea burst into full bloom. One of her horses was proving to be gentle and easy to train. She'd stood on his back and ridden around the corral. If she worked with him and Pal together, she might be able to have some real fun riding them both side by side, standing with one foot on each back. No time like the present.

She caught up the horse she had in mind—a beautiful blue roan that should have been treated as the special animal it was. She'd decided to call him Blue Boy. When she got through with him, anyone would be able to touch him. Not like that stupid horse of Preacher Powers. If he was a preacher. She sure wasn't convinced of it.

A glance at the sky later revealed she'd been out there for hours. Joanna would be wondering if she meant to help with the chores, and likely Toby needed dragging from the saloon before he could get falling-down liquored up.

She rode back to town, satisfied with the afternoon, and jumped from Pal's back in front of the saloon, glancing to the right and the left and over her shoulder. No sign of Powers. Annoyed with herself that she'd let him make her feel guilty, she pushed the swinging doors open and strode in.

Toby nursed a bottle.

She wondered if it was his first. But it was definitely his last. "Come on, Tobe. Time to leave."

He drained the bottle and wiped his mouth on his sleeve and gave her a bleary-eyed look bordering on defiance.

"Toby, I need your help." She'd long ago learned to make him think he did her a favor by leaving. She grabbed his hand and urged him to his feet.

He staggered, but she steadied him. It was her fault he was so far gone. She'd stayed with the horses too long.

Gently, she guided him to the door, swung the panels open with her hip, and half-dragged Toby through them. Her attention on keeping him going in a straight line, she wasn't watching where she went and bumped into someone holding the door ajar. "Sorry." She spared the man a glance and instantly her apology died. Powers. Could she never escape his challenging stare?

She gave him silent defiance for a full ten seconds then turned back to Toby and navigated him toward the stopping house, Pal in their wake. She had done nothing wrong. No reason she should feel guilty just because a man who called himself a preacher commented about the presence of a lady in the saloon. Like she'd told him, she was no lady. Following Pa from one frontier place to the next wild town had taught her to be otherwise.

Besides, who wanted to dress frilly and silly? Pretend to be weak and helpless so a man could run to her rescue? Not Glory Hamilton, that's for sure. She needed no man to rescue her or take care of her.

Somewhere in the back of her mind she remembered how Ma had tried to maintain a real home wherever they went. Joanna had taken over after Ma's death and did a fine job of being a mother. If she and Toby didn't get home and attend to their share of the chores mighty quick, Glory would be reminded in a very firm way that Joanna could reduce her to feeling like a child. "Hurry up, Toby. We're late."

He sucked in air. It seemed to clear his head or perhaps made him burn off some of the alcohol.

They reached the stopping house. Because they were late, Glory helped Toby carry in firewood. She intended to fill the box and get back outdoors before her sister could comment, but Joanna stopped her before she made her escape. "Glory, I need your help to run this place. But you know that."

"I'm sorry. I got busy with the horses."

Joanna sighed. "I figured as much, but it's a lot of work cleaning the place and cooking for a crew."

Glory nodded. "I'm sorry. I'll not do it again." She really didn't mean to leave Joanna with her share of the work, and she regretted she had. Life could be so complicated, and all because she'd taken time to do what she enjoyed most.

She grabbed up the ash bucket and dashed back outside. Joanna had set a sack of potatoes outside with knives and a big pot. Glory sat down on a rough stool, Toby at her side, and they quickly began to peel the potatoes.

"I saw you talking to Powers last night. You learn anything about the Rawhide Preacher?"

"Rawhide Kid," he corrected then paused and chortled, his foggy brain connecting his thoughts. "Oh, I get it. You mean because. . . Rawhide Preacher. I like it."

Glory guided his brain back to her question. "Did you learn anything?"

"He said he worked in a few towns as a preacher." He named them.

Glory had never heard of them, but that didn't mean anything. Towns sprang up in a matter of days where there had once been nothing but grass and trees. And she had no way of keeping up. Never had time to read a newspaper. And even if she had, the ones they got were old news.

Toby stopped peeling to explore his thoughts. " 'Course he could be lying. I've met many a good liar in my time."

"Me, too. Doesn't pay to believe everything a person says."

"Ain't that a fact?"

"What makes him think he can boss people around when you can't even trust what he says?" She whacked off a slice of potato and then, feeling guilty at the waste, popped it into her mouth.

"Uh-huh." Toby looked uncertain, as if not knowing what he had agreed to. " 'Course he did pray with some folk. Said grace real nice, too." Toby nodded vigorously. "And I heard him reading the Bible to some man."

Glory stifled an urge to roll her eyes. Toby made no sense,

but then what did she expect from someone she'd dragged from the saloon less than an hour ago?

But her own thoughts echoed Toby's arguments. She'd watched him care for Mr. Phelps, seen him washing out soiled laundry, spied on him taking things to Widow Kish. Glory had secreted away a few things each week for the woman, but it wasn't enough. Maybe with Powers helping, the woman would do better. Nice to know she had an ally in helping the widow. "Well, shoot!" She threw the peeled potato into the pot so hard she splashed Toby.

"What's wrong with you?"

"Nothing." How could she explain that one minute she tried to believe Powers was a fraud, and the next rejoiced he was a saint? Her mind must be affected by hanging upside down as she practiced her trick riding. But her horses were the safest company she could find right now, and she'd be spending a lot more time there and a lot less around town.

Except she needed to help Joanna. When did life get so complicated?

When the Rawhide Preacher rode into town. That's when. What would it take to get him to ride back out?

four

Levi would have thought it impossible for Glory to avoid
him, but she'd certainly done her best. Although they shared
the same table, so did twenty others, making it out of the
question to have a private conversation with her.

He wasn't sure what he'd say if he had the chance. He
thought of apologizing for suggesting she was disappointed
with life. Except he was almost certain it was the truth. The
outward signs might be different from Matt's—though not
all that different—but he suspected they both felt the same
way. Glory's mother had died. Her father left them to fend
on their own. It was almost as bad as losing both parents.
Perhaps even worse.

He'd watched for an opportunity to speak to her, prayed
for one, knowing without a shadow of doubt she was one
reason he was in Bonners Ferry. He'd even hung about the
farrier shop waiting for a chance, but she dragged young
Toby with her. He liked to think it was to keep Toby out of
the saloon, but deep down he suspected it was to make sure
she wasn't alone with Levi.

In a way, he didn't mind. Toby was welcoming enough, and
he liked the younger man. Right now they played a game of
checkers which seemed to be one of Toby's favorite pastimes.

Levi's gaze wandered back and forth to the open door,
which gave him a good view of the little pen and Glory
trimming hooves on the two horses brought to her.

"Now do a good job," the impatient man ordered. "I'm off
to the gold fields and can't afford a lame horse."

Glory didn't even glance up from her task. "Most foot problems can be prevented. You might try cleaning their hooves at night. They deserve that much after toting you around all day."

Levi held a bubble of amusement in his chest. Trust Glory to tell a man exactly what she thought.

Toby jumped Levi's kings. "I won."

Levi brought his attention back to the game. "So you did. You're pretty sharp for a young fella."

The boy bristled. "I'm not that young."

"Didn't mean to suggest you were."

Glory finished the horses and pocketed the money she'd earned. She let the man and his animals out the gate and then turned and began grooming her palamino.

Levi could see her lips moving but couldn't hear what she said to the horse. No doubt secrets she didn't share with others. He leaned toward the door, hoping to discover what they were.

"How old are you?" Toby asked.

Holding back his frustration, knowing Toby deserved his full attention, he answered. "Twenty-six. How about you?"

"I'm eighteen." He hung his head and mumbled. "Almost."

"I expect your folks are worried about you."

Toby bristled. "I can take care of myself."

"Don't stop your parents from wondering if you're okay. That's what folks do when they care about each other."

Glory suddenly stood in the doorway. "I suppose you know all about it? Folks caring and all."

He hadn't noticed her approach and startled, faced her. Their gazes met and held. And he saw one of her secrets. Though he already knew it. She had been disappointed by events in her life—likely her pa's regular disappearance and her mother's death. "My folks died when I was thirteen. My brother and I went to live with my grandparents. They cared for us in their own way." Trouble was, Matt didn't accept their way.

"What's that mean, 'their own way'?"

"They were strict but only because they feared we might get into trouble if we were allowed to follow our own inclination." They proved to be correct.

"So you think everyone should obey rules."

He hadn't meant for her to apply his words in such a fashion. "I only meant they showed their caring that way. The only way they knew how."

Her eyes blared like the sun had peeked around the corner and pooled in her irises. "Seems to me a man who calls himself a preacher would know love has certain requirements laid out in the scriptures. Perhaps you recall First Corinthians chapter thirteen, where it describes love as charity. Says it is long-suffering, kind, and never fails." Her words came fast and furious.

"Strange you pick those virtues when it also says charity vaunteth not itself, rejoiceth in the truth, and hopes all things." Stranger still she knew the passage. Yet perhaps not. Joanna made certain grace was offered at each meal so the girls had been exposed to godly teaching at some point in their lives.

She tried to stare him down, but he wasn't backing up, physically or mentally. When she realized he wouldn't budge, she made a noise of exasperation, grabbed the saddle and saddle blanket, and stomped outside. A few minutes later she rode down the trail at a gallop.

"She shouldn't ride so fast through town," Toby observed quietly. "Joanna is always telling her. But Glory doesn't listen."

No, Glory doesn't listen. That about summed it up.

❧

Sunday dawned clear and promising. *Thank You, Lord, for a nice day.*

One thing Levi had no control over was the weather, and meeting outdoors required good weather. He'd scoured the town looking for a suitable building to rent and had come up empty. All the buildings were in use.

He'd posted notices about town that he would hold services on the hillside south of the ferry. He'd announced it again at the supper table. Still he wondered how many would show up. Would Glory?

He took extra time with his grooming, aware of young Toby watching him.

"You really gonna have church outside?"

"Yup. Jesus held open-air services, you know." Levi finished his shave and wiped his face on the towel. As he finished and hung the towel, he caught a glimpse of Glory as she passed the open dining room door. "Are you coming?" He directed the question to Toby but hoped Glory heard it as well.

"Guess so. Glory says it might do me some good." The younger man hung his head and scuffled his feet. "She says maybe it will help me quit drinking." Suddenly he gave Levi a hard, demanding look. "You think it would?"

Levi gave the man his undivided attention. "Toby, going to church won't help you so much as listening to God will. God can give your life new purpose. He will forgive your sins and let you start over. Come to the service and hear what I have to say, and if you have other questions, I'm always willing to talk."

Toby brightened. "I'll be there."

Levi caught up his black suit jacket and donned it over his vest. Some might think it was an odd combination, but he didn't mind. Maybe they needed to see the preacher was more than a suit jacket. He was also a man. Did Glory see it?

Why did his thoughts always circle back to Miss Glory? Even at night, he recalled images of her—racing through town, scolding the man with horses, glaring at him across the table. Whether she smiled or glared, he derived a great deal of enjoyment out of picturing her.

He pushed the thought away. Today was not about him. Or her.

He picked up his Bible and headed for the field where the service was to be held. No one was there when he arrived. Nor did he expect it. It was a full hour before time to start. He'd come to pray and mentally prepare and welcome any early arrivals.

Half an hour later, people started to trickle in. Levi greeted each one. Claud Wagoner, whom he met the first day. Mr. Murray, the lawyer, and his wife. Widow Kish leaning on Mr. Phelps's arm.

Levi strode over and shook Mr. Phelps's hand and squeezed the widow's shoulder. "Glad to see you both. You're looking much better," he said to Mr. Phelps.

"Doing much better, thanks to you." He squeezed Levi's hand hard then released it and found a place for them to sit.

Others arrived. People he'd not yet met. A dozen people from the stopping house who decided to delay further travel until after the service. It was almost time to start. He swallowed back his disappointment. He'd hoped Glory and her sisters would come.

He took his place at the front and prepared to start the service.

At that moment, the three sisters strode down the path. Each wore her usual outfit—Mandy in loose pants and baggy shirt, Joanna in a split skirt and dark brown blouse, and Glory in tight britches, form-fitting shirt, and worn brown vest. But he had never seen anything he thought looked finer.

He smiled at them, his gazing skimming the older and younger sister and resting on Glory.

But she didn't return his smile. She scowled.

He turned away to face the gathered people, his smile widening. Her frown perhaps said more than a smile. It revealed the same uncertainty about her feelings for him as he had for her. He let the satisfaction of such knowledge fill his heart. Better to be frowned at than to be ignored.

"Welcome. We'll begin with a song." He didn't have hymnals but chose hymns familiar to most and led them in singing, pleased to hear some strong voices from the congregation. Mr. Phelps had a deep voice that carried the others along.

Then Levi began his sermon. He'd wanted to preach on rebellion being as the sin of witchcraft, or whatsoever a man soweth that shall he also reap. But he had no peace about such passages and instead chose others.

"Today, I want to remind each of you about God's everlasting love. In Jeremiah thirty-one, verse three, God says, 'I have loved thee with an everlasting love: therefore with loving kindness have I drawn thee.'" He went on to give illustrations from the scripture of God loving people even when they failed and sinned.

He tried not to speak directly to Glory though his heart strayed there on its own. She watched steadily. But her expression revealed nothing, giving him no idea whether the words spoke to her or not. But that was not his responsibility. God would use His Word in His way. Levi's task was to speak it.

Toward the end of the service, a large man sauntered to the edge of the clearing and leaned against a tree, his arms crossed over his chest. He plainly, silently said he wasn't there to hear from God.

Levi continued. "I want to remind you of the assurance in Numbers chapter twenty-three, verse nineteen. 'God is not a man, that he should lie; neither the son of man, that he should repent: hath he said, and shall he not do it?' and again in Joshua twenty-three, verse fourteen, 'Not one thing hath failed of all the good things which the Lord your God spake concerning you. . .not one thing hath failed therof.' God keeps His promises. I challenge you, read your Bible, find God's promises, trust them. 'O taste and see that the Lord is good: blessed is the man that trusteth in him.' Psalm thirty-four, verse eight."

He closed in prayer then moved to join the others, thanking them for attending and letting them know he was available for spiritual counsel or whatever they might need from him.

Many thanked him.

He sought Glory's eyes, wondering what she thought. More than once he felt he spoke directly to her, praying God would use his words to heal her hurt and disappointment. But she scrambled to her feet and seemed in a great hurry to get Joanna and Mandy to leave. However, they seemed more interested in speaking to their neighbors.

The late arrival still leaned against the nearby tree, a mocking expression on his face.

Levi strode over and introduced himself.

The man didn't unbend an inch. "I'm Bull Johnson."

"The saloon owner. I've been hoping to talk to you. I need a building for church services and thought you might be willing to let me use the saloon on Sunday."

Bull pushed away from the tree. He was big and brawny and used his body in a way meant to intimidate Levi.

Levi didn't budge an inch nor did he flinch. He'd met bigger, meaner men in his day. They didn't scare him. Big didn't make right.

Bull pushed his face to within an inch of Levi's. "Preacher, you stay away from my saloon on Sunday and every other day of the week. I won't have you interferring with my business."

Levi felt the silent watchfulness of his congregation. They waited to see how he'd react to this bully. He slowly drew himself to his full height, holding the Bible at chest level like a shield or perhaps a sword. "I will go where the Lord directs, when the Lord directs, and to whom the Lord directs. I will not fear any man when it comes to serving my Lord."

Bull edged closer, but Levi refused to move, forcing the man to teeter on the balls of his feet. He stepped back, a nasty look on his face. "Stay away from the saloon." He strode off, thunder in every footstep.

Levi turned away. Caught Glory's watchful look but could not read her expression. Admiration? He welcomed such. But perhaps it was only warning. Did she think him foolish for standing up to Bull? Or perhaps he only wanted to see something he could rejoice in. Could be she was only curious as any observer.

&

Glory tried to hurry Joanna and Mandy away from the church service. Levi tangled her thoughts with his words and actions. She'd come to the meeting fully expecting a fire-and-brimstone sermon. Warning about repentance and sackcloth. Instead, he preached love and trust. Neither of which she had any faith in.

Who was this Levi Powers? Seeing him help Mr. Phelps and Widow Kish, observing his fatherly way with Toby, and now hearing his words of welcome. . .well, it left her struggling for balance. Who was he?

Who was she? Did God really love her? She'd once believed. When Ma was alive. But it was so long ago she could barely recall, and she was but a child then, trusting her parents to take care of her.

That had changed, and she was no longer a child.

"I'm ready to go," Joanna said.

"Finally." Glory didn't bother to disguise her impatience.

Mandy nudged Glory in the ribs. "Still think he's too good-looking to be a preacher?"

Joanna shot them a startled look. "What's looks got to do with whether or not he's a preacher?"

Glory pinched Mandy's elbow, warning her not to josh with Joanna about it. Glory didn't much care to have another sister mocking her.

Mandy gave a naughty grin but said no more about the subject. She fell in on one side of Joanna and Glory on the other as they trooped toward home. The stopping house served only two meals a day—breakfast and supper—so the girls had the rest of the afternoon to themselves. No need to hurry back to the kitchen.

As they walked, Glory mulled over Levi's words. *"Read your Bible. Find God's promises."* Her voice careless, she asked, "Didn't Ma used to have a Bible? I wonder what happened to it."

"I've got it," Joanna said. "I think it's time I put it out so we can read it. I know Ma would have wanted us to." She sighed like she carried a heavy pack on her back. "Ma would be disappointed with me for not living up to her expectations."

"No, she wouldn't," Mandy and Glory said at once. Glory fell back half a step and cast a protesting look at Mandy. They'd seen Joanna get all worried and overly caring about how her younger sisters were turning out. She knew from

Mandy's expression she didn't welcome such a mood any more than Glory did.

"We're grown-up now," Glory said. "You don't have to worry about us so much." She vowed she would be more careful about how she acted and—she knew Joanna hated her going in the saloon even if it was to get Toby—where she went.

Joanna shrugged. "I will always feel responsible as the oldest."

"You've been the best big sister we could ask for. Isn't that right, Mandy?"

"Sure is." Both girls hugged Joanna who started to laugh.

"Still. I don't think it would hurt us any to read the Bible just as Levi said. Ma would want us to."

Glory didn't need to promise Joanna she would. Something deep in her soul wanted to know more about God's promises. Could He be trusted wholly and completely as Levi said? She sure hadn't found it easy to trust people. But then God was God. A different matter.

As soon as they got home, Joanna went to their room and lifted a box from the top shelf of the wardrobe. She opened it to reveal an old photo album and a tiny bonnet. "It was Mandy's. I've never been able to give it away." She set the album and bonnet aside. "Here's the Bible." Joanna stroked the worn leather cover gently. "Do either of you remember Ma reading to us from it?"

Glory nodded. "I remember her sitting in a rocking chair while we sprawled on the floor at her feet."

"I don't remember clearly," Mandy said. "I can never seem to remember Ma." She looked longingly at the photo album. Glory figured with Ma being sick so much when Mandy was little, her sister had learned to depend on Joanna for much of her care, and Ma kind of faded into the background for her.

Joanna sat on the edge of the bed, took the album on her lap, and patted the covers on either side of her. Glory and Mandy crowded close. It had been some time since they had shared a moment like this.

Glory knew what the pictures were. Grandparents she'd never met. Aunts and uncles she couldn't remember. Cousins no one could remember the names of. And Ma with Joanna as a toddler. Then Pa and Ma and the three girls, Mandy just a baby.

Joanna lingered over that page. "We were a good family."

Glory bristled. "We're still a good family. Just the three of us."

"What about Pa?" Mandy sounded mournful.

Glory didn't wait for Joanna to answer. She knew her sister would say Pa missed Ma. Never got over her dying. They had to understand that. But they had lost their ma, too. "We don't need Pa. Let him chase after his dreams. We manage just fine without him, don't we?"

Joanna stared into the distance as if seeing and wanting things she couldn't have.

Mandy sighed—a sound as sad as the wind off the river on a dark night.

Glory sprang to her feet. "I'm going to check on my horses." She sped from the house as fast as she could. But she couldn't outrun her thoughts. Pa would show up someday with the same empty promise of staying and providing a home for the girls. But they no longer needed him. Or wanted him and his promises—forgotten as quickly as they were given.

Promises. The word made her think of Powers's sermon. Maybe she needed to consider God's promises. Might be something there.

She spent the rest of the day with her horses, pleased at

how well Blue Boy and Pal worked together.

Later that evening, she sneaked into the bedroom, lifted Ma's Bible from the dresser where it now held center stage, ducked out the back door, avoiding her sisters and Powers, and found a secluded spot to read from its pages. There were promises galore. Surprised her some to see all the good things God promised to give. And it seemed they were meant for her, too.

Her back to a tree, the setting sun painting the river water violet, she tried to sort out her feelings. What if Powers was only a confidence man, with enough skill to convince them all he was a preacher?

Would that change God's promises?

No, it wouldn't. But it would change how she looked at the scriptures. Because, she reluctantly admitted, she heard the words in Levi's voice. And if he proved false, that wouldn't work.

Her instinct, her experience warned her to be cautious.

Her heart, her longing wished he could be all he said he was.

She closed the Bible and returned it to the dresser.

☙

Two days later, she left the horses early and headed back to town to get Toby and attend to their chores. She strode boldly into the saloon and looked about. No Toby. For the second day in a row. Yesterday she'd found him already at his chores, no smell of liquor on his breath. He explained he'd been too busy with other things to go to the saloon. But he refused to say what the other things were.

She rode slowly down the street, checking each corner and alley for a glimpse of Toby, fearing he had passed out somewhere. Not a sign of him. She neared the stopping house and saw nothing of him scurrying about the yard or perched under the overhang peeling vegetables.

It was early yet. Perhaps she'd missed him. She reined about and made another pass through town. Still not a sign of him. She rode on.

She neared Mr. Phelps's place and saw Levi's horse in front of the house and turned in there. Perhaps he'd seen Toby. She dismounted and led Pal toward the hitching post.

That was when she heard the murmur of voices and thought she recognized one as Toby's.

She edged around the corner of the house and stared. Levi Powers and Toby sat side-by-side, an open Bible between them. Mr. Phelps faced them. All three wore intent expressions.

Levi spoke. "It doesn't matter what we think or feel. It's what God's Word says that matters."

The other two nodded.

"And we just read where God says as far as the east is from the west He has removed our sins from us."

More nodding.

"If God says it, that settles it for me," Mr. Phelps said.

"Me, too," Toby echoed.

Glory backed away. So this was what kept Toby from the saloon. That was a good thing. So why did it feel like he'd betrayed her?

She returned to Pal and led him from the yard. Only someone selfish and petty would resent that her friend was being helped. And yet she did. In fact, her throat was tight. As if she wanted to cry.

She. . .Glory Hamilton. . .did not cry. Not when Pa rode away without a backward look. Not when Toby found what he needed from Levi. And not because she ached to be able to believe Levi was who he said he was. . .that she could trust his words.

Chomping down on her teeth until they hurt, she pushed away her foolish thoughts. She was glad for Toby.

And if she wanted to trust anyone, it would be God.

five

From the doorway where Glory stood drying the heavy pot Joanna used to cook porridge in, she could see the comings and goings on the ferry. Another busy day of people flocking to the gold fields of the British territories, to some mysterious place called the Kootenais.

She and her sisters had planned to find Pa and join him there until they saw the opportunity to make a good living by running a stopping house. Mandy had wanted to push on and join Pa. But Joanna and Glory outvoted her.

Glory liked it here. Perhaps they would stay for a long time. She thought of the land she hoped to purchase.

A big black horse riding toward the ferry caught her attention. Levi's horse. She'd recognize it anywhere. Just as she'd recognize the man riding it. The relaxed yet watchful way he sat his horse. His proud posture. The fringed leather vest so out of place for a preacher. Rawhide Kid seemed a more fitting title.

He rode his horse to the ferry and crossed the river.

Toby appeared at her side.

"Where is he going?" she asked.

"Didn't say."

"Just rode off without a word?"

Toby continued to look at Levi. "Said he felt an urge to cross the river and see if anyone needed his help."

They watched until Levi rode out of sight on the far side of the river.

Glory shifted her gaze to Toby and for some inexplicable

reason was annoyed. "I wonder if he's off looking for people to help. More likely to help himself to their things. Have you forgotten the Rawhide Kid? He could be a fake. Remember?"

Toby took his time turning to face her. "He knows about God."

Glory's eyes narrowed, and her heart squeezed hard. Toby was her friend. Yet he was choosing to believe Levi over Glory. "You believe him?"

Toby gave the merest shrug.

Glory's insides tightened until she wondered something didn't snap. "I thought you were my friend."

"I am. What does believing Levi have to do with being your friend?"

She couldn't answer because nothing made sense. "Forget it." She spun away and headed for her shop.

In minutes she had saddled Pal and rode out of town to her horses. At least horses were loyal to anyone who treated them right.

Recognizing she was too upset to work with the animals at the moment, she plunked down in her favorite spot, her back to a tree, and looked out at the wide, green valley below. She never grew tired of the view, and slowly her thoughts calmed.

Why had she gotten so upset? It wasn't like she needed Toby's friendship. She had learned many years ago not to get too attached to friends.

Nor did she resent the time he spent with Levi. She was glad his association with the man kept him out of the saloon.

Deep inside the truth sought acceptance. She was—

No. She didn't ache for Levi to show her the same kindness and attention. She didn't long for friendship from him. No way. That was silly nonsense. Why would she pin her hopes on a man? Any man. She'd learned the folly of such at a young age.

She sprang to her feet and returned to her horses. As

she fed them and petted them, her good humor returned. This was who she was and where she belonged. Nothing else mattered. Silly to let other things upset her for even a moment.

Pal and Blue Boy worked perfectly together. They were ready and there was no time like the present. She'd do it today. Excitement filled her insides with rolling whitecaps like those blown up on the river by a strong westerly wind.

She rode Pal and led Blue Boy until she reached the beginning of the street running down to the ferry. "This is it, boys." She pulled them to a halt, clambered from the saddle, and put one foot on the back of each horse, finding perfect balance before she flicked the reins for them to go forward.

She was in complete control. The feeling was powerful, pulsing through her veins in sweet victory. She held the reins in one hand and punched the air with her free hand. "Whaahoo," she called.

Several men crossing the street stopped to stare, the surprise on their faces fueling her excitement. Two more men crowded through the door of the hardware store at the same time, anxious to see.

"Look, Ma," a young boy called. His mother stared, one hand holding her son firmly at her side.

Glory rode down the street, grinning so widely her cheeks hurt. She reined in before she reached the stopping house, preferring not to have Joanna see her, then turned and rode back through town.

A familiar figure stood in front of the general store. Joanna. Glory's heart thudded against her chest. Wasn't Joanna supposed to be home cooking up something? Instead, she gave Glory a look full of reproach.

Glory faltered. The horses felt it and broke their pace, setting her off balance. She struggled to hold her footing.

"Pal, Blue Boy, it's okay."

Suddenly Levi stood directly in front of the horses and grabbed each by the bridle.

"Let them go." Glory stood atop motionless horses, feeling slightly foolish. She was supposed to ride from town without a hitch.

"Get down." His eyes blazed brittle blue. His words, though low, had the power of a gunshot.

"No. Release my horses."

"Glory, get down before you hurt yourself."

Anger flared through her, burning away every rational thought. She dropped to the ground in one swift motion and flung to his side. "You ought to mind your own business."

"And you ought to behave yourself." His voice dropped even lower. "Did you see the look on your sister's face? You scared her. She cares about you. Do you think it's fair to worry her like this?"

She did silent, vicious battle with her eyes. He had no right to interfere. But then she hadn't intended for Joanna to see. Yes, she would hear about it eventually, but after it was over and done and Glory could laugh and say there'd been no risk involved.

Out of the corner of her eyes, she saw Joanna striding toward her. She yanked Pal's bridle from Levi's hand, but he refused to release Blue Boy. Knowing if she didn't make tracks she'd have to face Joanna, she headed down the street. Like a shamed dog with her tail between her legs.

He kept stride with her, bringing Blue Boy along.

"You humiliated me in public. I'll never forgive you for that."

☙

Levi held his tongue because the words wanting to burst from his mouth would not be God-honoring. He wanted to tear her apart for such a foolish act. When the horses had faltered and it looked like she would fall, he'd stopped thinking and acted on sheer instinct. All he wanted was to keep her from getting hurt.

And for that she vowed she would never forgive him.

A whirlwind of emotions swept through him. Relief she was on the ground walking on two sound legs. Though he wasn't sure his legs were so sound. His knees were strangely wobbly. He recognized it as the aftereffects of his scare. "Are you crazy or something? You could have been killed."

She made a most unladylike sound. "I was in complete control."

"Of everything, I suppose. People who might inadvertently step into the street and startle the horses or some sudden noise. Sure you were in control. I suppose you were in control of the shock it gave Joanna, too."

She glared at him. "She wasn't supposed to be there."

"That makes no sense. How would it worry her less if she hadn't seen it?"

"What she doesn't know won't hurt her."

"Your shenanigans only give her cause to worry all the more when she can't see what you're up to. Don't you stop to give a thought to those who care about you? Don't you care about yourself?" He dropped back, too upset to continue walking with her. "I'm going to check on Mr. Phelps."

She pulled to a halt in front of the man's yard facing him, anger and defiance wreathing her face.

He stared at her as truth surfaced. He'd worried she might do something lawless like Matt had. But that was not the risk she faced. Her defiance would lead her to put herself in danger with no regard for the consequences. "Why are you so determined to prove nothing matters to you?"

She glared at him, her eyes flashing. "Because it doesn't."

She blinked as if realizing what she'd said. "I am not foolish."

He grabbed her by the shoulders and gave a little shake. "You are indeed foolish if you think you don't matter to anyone. Or nothing you do matters to them."

Her gaze bored into his, probing, testing, wanting. Then she scowled. "What do you know about it?"

"I know this. I care what happens to you. I care about you."

Disbelief filled her eyes.

He saw an argument about to start. He didn't care to have his confession debated and pulled her close, tipped her chin up, and silenced her with a good, solid kiss. Her lips siffened with what he presumed was shock. He knew he should stop, back away, behave like a gentleman, but he allowed himself a moment more of sweet tasting then pulled away. "Never argue with a man when he says he cares about you."

She stared.

He turned away to hide his smile. If he had to guess, he'd say it was the first time in her life Glory had been rendered speechless.

❧

Levi hummed as he waved good-bye to Mr. Phelps. He'd spent a pleasant half hour visiting and now headed back to town.

When he saw the ferry, he remembered what he'd found on the other side. . .what had bothered him since he returned.

Two children, a boy and a girl, sitting by the side of the road.

"Waitin' for our pa," the boy said. "He said he'd be back for us."

Levi had hunkered down beside the pair. "How long have you been waiting?" He thought they'd say an hour, maybe most of the day. But what they said shot through him like a bullet.

"Been three days now," the boy said, and the little girl sobbed quietly.

"Maybe you should wait back in town. I could take care of

you until he gets back."

The little girl's eyes widened with hope, but her brother shook his head. "I promised Pa I'd stay here."

He gave them the biscuits and jerky he had with him and refilled their water canteens then headed back to town. "The offer is open if you change your mind." It troubled him to leave them there, but he didn't want to forceably remove them. How would he explain dragging two screaming children into town?

Perhaps their father had returned by now. *God, keep them safe. Bring their father back to them. Guide me as to what I should do.*

He spent the day visiting various people. But his thoughts returned over and over to Glory and the kiss he'd stolen. He went back to the stopping house more eagerly than usual. He could hardly wait to see her at the evening meal. See if her cheeks flushed when she saw him.

She clattered into the dining room and crowded in next to Mandy. "Sorry I'm late," she murmured.

Levi had seen her earlier peeling potatoes and doing the other chores that seemed to be her responsibility, Toby assisting her. The boy had stopped going to the saloon. Not something Bull appreciated, but Levi was pleased.

He stood to say the blessing as had become his habit then sat and waited for Glory to glance his way. She made a great show of being busy with passing the food. He grinned. Avoiding him proved more than an angry glare would have, and he turned his attention to the man on his right to answer a number of questions.

"Could you please pass me the salt?" the man on his left asked.

As Levi turned to do so, he looked toward Glory and caught her watching him, her expression serious, guarded. Yet the hunger in her eyes made him forget what he was doing until the man spoke again.

"The salt, please."

He passed the salt and directed his attention to his plate. Suddenly the impact of what he'd done hit him. What was he thinking? He had no business telling Glory he cared. His task required all his time and attention. And he silently repeated the vow he had made to God. *I'll devote myself to working for You while You work on Matt in prison. Keep him safe. Bring him to repentance.*

After the meal, he joined the others outside, but he listened to Glory cleaning up the meal inside. She usually left the house after the chores and disappeared until dark. He'd watched her. Saw she carried a Bible. Guessed she found a quiet place to read it, and he rejoiced in the fact. He didn't like to interrupt her reading, but tonight he would follow her and apologize for kissing her. Not that he was sorry. But he had no business.

He knew the moment she slipped from the house even though he didn't hear her or see her. His heart tracked her as she crossed the yard and ducked into a thicket of trees. Giving her a moment to settle, Levi excused himself from the knot of men visiting and sauntered away, choosing an indirect route. As he neared the trees, he called softly, "Glory, I need to speak to you." Then he hastened forward before she could escape.

She sat with her back against a tree, the dappled light making it difficult to read her expression. "Can't a person enjoy some peace and quiet without you interrupting?" And she turned her attention to the Bible in her lap, pointedly ignoring him.

There wasn't room to lean against the same tree, and she made it clear she didn't welcome closeness, so he chose the next tree over and sat down, his legs sprawled out in front of him. He took in a deep, satisfying breath. "I won't keep you. I only want to apologize. I shouldn't have kissed you. Or said those things."

"You're taking it all back?"

He considered his answer a moment and could find nothing better to say than, "Seems the best thing to do."

"Not surprised." She spoke so quietly he wondered if he'd misunderstood her.

"What do you mean? It isn't like I've done this before."

She shrugged, looked as if she didn't intend to answer then sighed. "Not you. Others have though."

"Others?" He didn't want to think other men had stolen kisses. Or worse, been given them. "How many beaus are we talking about?"

She gave him a scowl fit to dry up the river. "Not beaus. I got no use for that nonsense."

"Then who?"

"My pa. Not that it's any of your business, but he's a great one for saying something then changing his mind."

Levi digested the information. It appears it was her father who disappointed her. "What did he do?"

A heavy sigh pushed past her lips. "It was what he didn't do."

"Alright. What didn't he do?"

She slowly turned and fixed him with a look full of defiance but also laced with regret and longing.

He ached to be able to comfort her, but he didn't have the right. Would never have the right.

"He couldn't be bothered to be a father. It interfered with his plans."

He held her gaze, reading past the anger to the pain. "I'm sorry. However, I am not your pa. Nor do I wish to hurt you. I care about you, but I don't have the right." He gathered his feet beneath him and stood. "I will never have the right." He strode away, not daring a backward glance. He had set his face to the plough and would not look back.

The next day he would again cross the river on the ferry and ride to where he'd last seen the children, hoping they were gone—safely with their father. Hoping they had not been bothered by someone with less than noble intentions.

The morning couldn't come too soon for him.

six

Glory forced herself not to toss and turn, knowing it would bring questions from Joanna and Mandy. Instead, she curled on the far side of the bed she shared with her younger sister and stared into the darkness.

Of course Levi didn't mean what he said. Why had she expected he would? She was no more than twelve when she realized words were easily given and just as easily taken back.

Her Pa had taught her well. Every year—sometimes several times in a year—he'd promised he'd stay with the girls this time. And every time he rode out of their lives, most times without warning or good-bye.

She'd lost track of the number of times they'd been thrust upon the care of others until they rebelled. Joanna was sixteen, almost seventeen, when they'd convinced her they could manage on their own. As a trio, they'd tried to keep up with Pa, depending on him to give them a home. But they got tired of that real quick. Seems the more he saw of them, the more he wanted to move on. Still, they tried to stay close. After all, he was their pa. They learned to manage on their own, hunting, fishing, cooking, cleaning, tending children. . . whatever it took to survive.

She firmly pushed regrets to the back of her mind. That was the past and there was no benefit in moaning about what might have been. They now had their own successful business. It should have been enough for all of them and it was, but besides helping run the stopping house, Glory wanted to take care of abused or neglected horses, nursing them back to health.

She thought of the tin can under her side of the bed where she kept her earnings. How long would it take before she had enough to buy that piece of land?

By the time morning dawned, she could hardly wait to be up and about her chores. She hurried through them, barely taking time to stop for breakfast.

Somehow she managed to keep her gaze from roving toward Levi. Kiss her and regret it would he? Well, she didn't need the likes of him. She was drying the last dish when she saw him on the ferry, again crossing the river, and her suspicions mounted. He said he would never be free to care for her. That wasn't quite the word he'd used. The right. He'd never have the right. Whatever that meant. But if he was part of a gang, involved in robbery or other illegal activity, wouldn't it mean he didn't have the right?

Was he the Rawhide Kid posing as a preacher? She didn't like to think so, but it made perfect sense.

She wished it didn't.

As soon as she recognized the thought, she wanted to boot herself across the yard. What difference did it make to her? None. None whatsoever. She was only thinking of how many people would be disillusioned when they discovered the truth. She was above and beyond disappointment. That was one good thing her pa had taught her.

As soon as she'd done her share of chores, she returned to the horses. A pleased grin curved her mouth. She'd ridden the horses in tandem. It gave her a great deal of satisfaction.

Simply for the sheer fun of it, she stood on the backs of the pair and rode them around the pasture. She did the death drag from Pal's back. The thrill of the trick blew away all her troubles.

After she had enough, she turned her attention to the big gray gelding. Today she was determined to get him to let her touch him. She shook some oats into her hat and slowly approached the animal. He quivered but didn't snort and race away. He liked his oats too much.

She laughed softly as he allowed her to close the distance between them. His nostrils quivering, he reached for the oats, but she kept them close to her body. "If you want them, you'll have to forget your fear of me."

The big animal shook his head, but his gaze returned to the oats and he jerked forward, almost reaching them, but he shivered away without so much as a taste.

"Take it easy, big fella. I won't hurt you. In fact, you might find you like having me touch you." She shook the hat, reminding him of the waiting treat. "Oats. See? You know how much you like them."

Slower, but still cautious, he stretched out his neck and managed to lick up a few grains.

"Not enough to satisfy you, is it? Come on, forget about the past and people who have hurt you. I'm different. I won't hurt you. You can trust me."

The horse eased forward and suddenly buried his nose in the hat, forcing Glory to hang on with both hands. She rested the hat against her stomach and gently, gently touched his neck. He quivered but didn't pull away from the oats.

Glory laughed softly. "See, it's not so scary after all." She touched him again, thrilling at this victory.

He snuffled up the last of the oats and trotted away to watch her from a safe distance.

Glory couldn't stop grinning. "You and I are going to be great friends once you learn you can trust me."

Trust. She knew it took a long time to prove to an abused animal trusting was okay. Her thoughts filled with questions from her past and promises from God's Word, entwined together like a ball of knotted yarn. She sat in her favorite spot to consider the tangle.

Levi had said he cared and then changed his mind.

She wasn't sure he was a preacher or a crook. Plain and simple, she didn't trust him. And yet he said to search the Bible and find God's promises. He assured them all they could trust those promises.

She thought of some of the ones that had found their way into her heart. A promise to love her—*"I have loved thee with an everlasting love"*—a promise to hear when she called on Him, to draw near to her, to answer her requests. Dare she trust Him?

The words that Levi had brought that first Sunday came to mind. *"God is not a man, that he should lie; neither the son of man, that he should repent: hath he said, and shall he not do it? or hath he spoken, and shall he not make it good?"* The next Sunday he had given even more promises from God's Word, but she wasn't sure she was ready to thrust herself wholly into someone else's care. Not even God's. Life had disappointed too often for trust to come readily.

A horse approached, and she scrambled to her feet.

The man drawing near was a stranger. In a fine suit. With a round-topped black hat that looked like it had just been plucked out of a store display. He rode well, though in a stiff manner. Not like a cowboy who spent hours in a saddle. He drew to a halt before her. "You are on my land."

Not now. Her heart reached bottom and lay there limp. She'd hoped this day would never come. "Who are you?"

He pulled off his hat to reveal blond hair slicked back with plenty of pommade. "Master Marcus Milton." He returned his hat to his head and looked almighty pleased with himself, as if she should rejoice at meeting such a fine, pompous man.

She bit the inside of her lip in order to keep her opinion to herself.

When he realized she didn't plan to comment on the privilege of meeting Master whatever, he gave a decisive nod. "Do you have plans to purchase this land?"

"How much?"

He named a sum likely fair enough but far more than she had in her tin can. Even selling her current half-dozen horses wouldn't bring in enough money. "I could pay part now and part later."

He sniffed. "I am a businessman. Borrow the money from a bank. In the meantime, either buy the land or move your horses off it."

"They're not hurting anything."

"You're trespassing."

"I need time to find another suitable location. After all, I can't keep them tied up in town, now can I?"

"Very well. I am a reasonable man." He looked like it pained him to say so. "I will give you two weeks." He beamed at her.

She stared, suddenly realized he expected her to thank him. "You'll have your money in less time than that."

"Or you will remove your animals." He jerked his mount around.

It was all Glory could do not to order him to keep in mind the horse's tender mouth. She watched him until he disappeared from sight then sank back to the ground and moaned. "How am I supposed to get that kind of money in less than two weeks?" Dare she pray about it? Would God listen to a foolish, selfish request? What did she have to lose?

God, help me out here if You care about me at all. You say in Your Word You care. But everyone who says they care about me takes it back one way or the other. But You aren't a man to change Your mind. So if it's true, if I can trust You, make a way for me to buy this piece of land.

She didn't say amen. Just finished and sat there, a little kernel of hope sprouting.

Later, she returned to town, curious as to whether or not Levi was back. Or was he out taking advantage of innocent people? Perhaps even planning to rob a bank or something equally as dreadful. Her mistrust of Levi was at such odds with the step of trust she'd taken up the hill. But trust did not come easily, and she'd learned it shouldn't be given freely.

She half-expected to see Levi striding into the saloon, despite Bull's continued threats and warnings. Once she'd seen Bull pushing him out the door, growling and saying all kinds of horrible things, but Levi seemed to be hard of hearing. Why would he even bother going there when he knew it meant nothing but trouble from Bull? Was it part of a ruse? Or for real? She wished she knew. But it didn't make any difference to her. Not really. He couldn't or wouldn't care about her. And she didn't care about him.

There was no sign of him at the saloon. She stopped and dismounted, checked to see if Toby was inside. He wasn't. Maybe the two of them were together someplace, though she'd seen no sign of Levi's big horse outside Mr. Phelps's house. Not that she had looked. She was only being observant.

She swung back into the saddle and headed for her shop. Sometimes he sat on the step talking to Toby as they waited for her. No one sat on the step. No one waited for her.

And why had she expected anyone would? It was only because she was angry at him for saying something he didn't mean. Just proved he was like every other man she knew.

She unsaddled Pal and turned him into the pen. Time to head to the stopping house and take care of the chores.

Toby was already there, already had the wood box full and the ashes cleaned out and was about to tackle the bucket of potatoes as she approached.

She sat on the bench and started peeling a wrinkled potato. "What have you been doing today?" It was normal conversation. No reason to feel all jittery about asking such a question. She stifled a desire to groan. It wasn't the question that bothered her. It was the curiosity behind it. *Where is Levi?*

"Been hanging about waiting for Levi to get back."

"Where did he go?"

"Only thing he said was he had something to attend to up the trail."

"That doesn't make a lick of sense. Is he trying to make us think he has legitimate business?"

"Maybe."

"He's got you convinced he's really a preacher, hasn't he?" She pointed out he was the first one to suggest the Rawhide Kid. After hearing him preach again each Sunday, she was almost ready to believe it. Almost.

"Glory, you should talk to him. Then you'd be convinced, too."

"I've talked to him, and it surely didn't convince me."

He stopped peeling potatoes to study her. "What did he say to upset you so much?"

"Enough for me not to trust him."

He returned to his task. "You'll see sooner or later."

"I expect I shall." As usual, she sat so she could see the comings and goings on the ferry. And not—she informed herself—because she hoped to glimpse Levi returning without a posse on his tail.

The vegetables were prepared, the table set when she saw him on the ferry. Or at least she saw an animal like his horse. But this man had two children with him. Where did he get two children? He hadn't killed their parents in a robbery or kidnapped the children hoping for a ransom, had he?

He rode slowly toward the stopping house. At the hitching post, he reached behind him and swung a small boy to the ground. Then he lifted the child from in front of him and leaned over to deposit that one beside the first.

Glory stepped from the dining room to watch.

A small boy with a defiant look on his face clutched the hand of a smaller girl who looked as if she'd been crying recently.

Levi swung to the ground and pushed his hat back on his head in a gesture speaking worry and confusion better than any words could have.

She crossed the porch and faced him squarely. "Where did you get these children?"

He grinned as if reading her suspicious thoughts. "I didn't steal them, and I know that's what you're thinking. I found them. Rescued them." He told of finding the pair at the side of the road, waiting for their father to return. Waiting for four days without losing hope.

Their fear and pain drew deep lines in both little faces. It was too much like her own experience, and Glory had to turn away, pretending an interest in something inside the dining room while she gathered up her self-control. "You couldn't just bring home a lost dog like everyone else. Oh no, you have to find two lost children."

"We weren't lost," the boy protested. "Was waitin' for our pa. He won't be happy we didn't stay where he told us to. But"—his sigh was half shudder and perilously close to a sob—"we was getting hungry and tired and my sister was afraid. We could hear the coyotes howling so close at night."

Glory pressed her lips together and stilled her emotions. These children were even younger than she had been and without a protective older sister. She looked at Levi in silent protest, hoping he saw nothing but shock and dismay that these children had been abandoned.

Levi's expression revealed an equal amount of both plus a

healthy dose of anger. "It took me all afternoon to persuade them to come with me."

The little girl stuck out her chin in an act of such defiance Glory had to press her lips together to keep from smiling. "He said he'd take care of us and find our pa."

Glory shook her head as she turned back to Levi. "Sounds like a mighty big task."

He shrugged. "How hard can it be? Besides, I couldn't leave them there another day. I doubt you could have either."

She forced all emotion from her eyes and answered cooly. "I suppose not. After all, they are just children."

The boy widened his stance. "I'm Jack Templeton. This is my sister, Emmy. I can take care of her."

Glory recognized his determination and admired it. "How old are you?"

"Ten." A boy with a tangle of straw-colored hair and brown eyes. "Emmy's—"

"I'm eight." Similar in looks to her brother, only her hair was longer and her eyes wider and filled with forced bravery. And as afraid as any child.

Glory straightened and met Levi's eyes. "What are you going to do with them?"

"Exactly what I said. Take care of them and try to locate their father."

She nodded and without another word went back inside. She went directly to the kitchen where Joanna and Mandy waited.

"What's going on?" Joanna asked.

"He found two kids." She repeated his story.

Joanna sighed. "Familiar story, wouldn't you say?"

Mandy moved to the doorway so she could watch them. "He's washing them up. The little girl is so tiny. She looks up at him with big trusting eyes." Mandy's words choked. "I can't imagine leaving such a sweet pair behind."

Glory snorted. "What? Were we ugly? And even if we were, did that make it alright for Pa to leave us time and again?"

"I'm sure he didn't mean to. He just got busy."

"Mandy, when will you learn we just didn't matter to him? Still don't, if one goes by the evidence." She waved her hands to indicate the room. "You see him here? Did he tell us where he was going? No. I say forget about him and get on with our lives."

"Hush, girls." Joanna as always played the peacemaker. "We are doing the best we can. All of us. Only time and God's love will heal some wounds."

Glory and Mandy exchanged surprised looks then faced Joanna who laughed awkwardly.

"Ma taught us to obey God and trust Him. I guess it's about time we all did."

"I'm trying," Glory mumbled.

"I feel close to God when I'm out in the woods." Mandy sounded confused.

Joanna patted them both on the back. "We need to look to the future, not the past." She sniffled and wiped her eyes on a corner of her apron. "Now let's serve our guests."

Glory helped carry in the full platters and mounded bowls. Not until the food was on the table did Joanna signal at the door for the guests to come in. As they filed by, they dropped their coins into her hand.

Glory watched as Levi dropped in coins for three.

He looked tired and worried as he found room for himself with a child on each side. But Emmy trembled when a strange man sat beside her.

Glory caught Levi's eyes and signalled to him to check the child at his elbow.

He did so, saw how frightened she was, and changed places with her so she sat between himself and Jack. He glanced to Glory, said a silent thank-you.

She turned away, pretending she didn't notice. It was almost more than she could do to watch his tenderness with the children. She forced steel into her thoughts. Would he tell them the same thing he'd told her? That he couldn't care about them and that he took back his promise?

She was quite prepared to ignore the three of them. But against her will, her gaze returned to them over and over, watching as Levi cut Emmy's meat, as he refilled their water glasses. Like a father with his children.

Determinedly, she closed her eyes. She would not be like Mandy, always hoping Pa would return and somehow be changed into an ideal father. Nor would she look for the tenderness and caring she'd missed from her father in some other man. She understood how even a whisper of that kind of thinking made her vulnerable to more hurt and disappointment. The best thing she could do would be to stay as far away as possible from Levi and these two little ones until such time as he reunited them with their father.

A thought ached through her. What if they didn't find the missing father? Seems if a man didn't want to be found, he had a hundred different ways of disappearing.

As soon as the meal ended, she hurried to the kitchen to start washing dishes, determined she would not watch what Levi did with the children. Not that she had to. Mandy gave a running account.

"He's making sure they wash up again." "He's sitting on the bench outside with them. Looks like he's telling them a story. Both children are staring at him with such big eyes they practically eat him up."

Glory could take no more. "I don't want to hear about him."

Mandy laughed. "You're jealous because he's spending time with those kids. You want him to spend time with you. I saw him follow you into the trees the other evening. And why is he always hanging around the farrier's shop? Not because he has dozens of horses to take care of."

Glory threw the wet dishrag into the water with a splash and spun around to face her sister. "That's stupid talk. You be quiet."

Mandy wrinkled her nose. "I will say what I want."

"No, you won't." Glory jumped for her, intending to forceably shut her mouth, but Mandy guessed her intent and raced out of the house.

"You can't stop me." She laughed as Glory tore after her.

"When I catch you, you'll be sorry. I'll hurt you real bad."

Mandy had always been faster than Glory, but Glory was more desperate, more angry, and she did not give up the chase for half a mile. Finally, winded and knowing she didn't have a chance of catching her sister, Glory ground to a halt. "You have to come back sometime," she shouted.

Mandy stopped to face her, a good distance separating them. "You have to stop being mad sometime."

Glory laughed. Her anger had already fled.

She marched back to the house, humming to herself, and stared at Emmy, watching her with wide-eyed fear. She shifted. Saw how Jack looked ready to flee. She recalled her threatening words, the anger that no doubt had been evident on her face, and wished she could recall the past few moments and do them over.

Although she vowed she would not look at Levi, her eyes somehow shifted his direction and their gazes collided. His look burned. Accused.

"Nice example," he murmured.

Two seconds ago she'd been wishing she'd acted differently.

Not frightened the children. Now she wished she'd caught Mandy and wrestled her to the ground just to prove to Levi she didn't care a thing about his opinion.

"You were mad," Emmy whispered.

Glory's stubbornness warred with her concern for two innocent children. The latter won out. "Only for a moment. My sister knows that. It's a game we like to play."

"You shouldn't say bad things."

Glory grinned at the little girl. "So I'm told." She flounced around and headed for the kitchen to finish her chores.

Joanna watched her return. "Will you ever learn to be a lady?"

Glory gave her an unrepentant smirk. "When you do."

Joanna glanced down at her split skirt and laughed. "I'm as ladylike as I can be. No wonder they call us the buffalo gals."

"It could be a lot worse." They grinned at each other. "I'm happy enough to be a buffalo gal."

"Me, too."

Mandy returned a little later, and the three girls worked in happy contentment.

At bedtime, Levi found a corner and bedded the two children down at his side.

Glory tried to ignore them, but it was impossible not to hear him reading aloud from the Bible then see him kneeling with them to say their prayers. He tucked the covers around them firmly.

Glory could almost feel the comfort of those blankets holding her close. He wasn't even their father. Why was he acting like he was? Did some men simply react to children in a tender way?

She fled to the bedroom she shared with her sisters. Mandy was wrong. She wasn't jealous. She didn't want him to give her the same kind of attention. Yet there was no denying the long, echoing ache inside her yearning for something.

seven

Levi lay back on his bedding and let out a long sigh of relief. It had been a difficult afternoon. The children didn't want to disobey their father and leave the spot where he'd told them to wait. They flat out refused until Levi said he would scratch a message in the rock at the side of the road. It had taken him a long time to do so. But that gave him an opportunity to explain how he would send a message up the line and see if they could locate their pa. He talked about the good meals at the stopping house and the nice ladies who ran it.

Eventually, they agreed to come but only after checking and approving the message on the rock. He'd gathered up their sack of belongings—a few items of clothing and one set of bedding he knew they shared, likely clinging to each other for security and warmth.

He hadn't taken into account the variety of men who clustered around the table morning and night. Some fine gentlemen. But also some rough characters. After supper, Emmy confessed they scared her. Levi didn't know what else to do. He had no home. And knew of none suitable to keep them in. The hotel certainly wasn't. The men he'd seen leaving that place convinced him it was not fit for decent people.

Staying with the buffalo gals seemed the best idea except it brought him back to the initial problem—Emmy was uncomfortable among so many strange men. And he didn't want to be forced by such circumstances to spend more time with Glory. His wayward thoughts far too often drifted toward her, recalling his pleasure when he kissed her, remembering how she challenged a man about how he treated his horses, how she—

No, he must keep his hands and mind to the task before him. He had made a bargain with God and intended to keep it.

The men around him settled down. There was a constant sound of shuffling and snoring, but he was too tired to be bothered by it. He silently prayed for God to help him find the children's father then rolled over and fell asleep.

A scream jolted him awake. He reached for his rifle, found only bare wood. Felt about him, remembering he slept in the stopping house and his rifle was with his saddle and other things. He sat up as did several others. Someone lit a lamp and held it high.

A bewiskered man who had spat out a steady stream of black tobacco juice all evening bolted to his feet, revealing a very dirty undershirt. He grabbed the lamp and shone it into every corner of the room. "Who screamed?"

The flickering yellow light stopped at Emmy who sat up, tears streaming down her face, and as everyone stared at her, her sobs grew loud.

Jack pushed from his slumber and reached out for his sister. "You had a nightmare. Go back to sleep."

She didn't move.

Levi urged her to lie down. Covered her tightly. Patted her back gently, murmuring soft sounds. "It's all over, folks. Go back to sleep."

But he spoke too soon. He had no sooner fallen asleep again when another scream rent the air.

"Make her stop," someone called in the dark.

"I'm trying to get some rest," another growled.

Murmurs and snarls came from various corners.

Levi again soothed the child. When he heard her soft, steady breathing, he allowed himself to fall back asleep.

But again his peace was shattered by Emmy's screams.

The protests from the other guests grew louder, more abusive.

Levi knew it would be impossible for him to sleep if he meant to keep the child quiet. He pulled on his trousers, scooped Emmy into his arms, and escaped outside. He got as comfortable as possible on one of the narrow benches, resting his back against the rough wooden wall, wrapped one of his blankets about Emmy, and settled down for a restless night.

Twice more she cried out, loud enough to bring a muttering of protests from inside.

Finally dawn eased across the hills and turned the air pink. Geese came awake on the river, honking in joyful song. Birdsong filled the air. So peaceful. Why couldn't man enjoy nature and stop hurting themselves and each other?

Inside came the sound of one of the women—likely Joanna—in the kitchen, rattling pots on the stove. And men started to surface from their sleep.

Two men passed him, muttering about how their night had been so disturbed.

Jack came out and sat by Levi. "She was scared being with so many strangers."

"I know."

He felt Emmy stir, knew she wakened. But she seemed content to remain curled in his arms. And he was too weary to move.

One by one, or in pairs, the men left the room to allow breakfast to be set out. Not a one had a kind word about Emmy's upset. All they seemed to care about was their disturbed sleep.

"I'm hungry," Jack said.

"Did you roll up your bedding?"

"Uh-huh."

"Bring your things and mine out to the porch then wash up."

Emmy sighed, sat up, and rubbed her eyes.

Levi took her to wash.

"Breakfast is ready," Glory called and stepped aside to allow the men to reenter. Joanna waited to take their coins.

The crude man from the night before stepped forward. "I don't intend to pay for a night when I wasn't allowed to sleep. I want my money back."

Others crowded about him, and their discontent rumbled.

Glory pressed to Joanna's side. She gave Levi a look full of accusation.

He didn't need her to silently inform him this was his fault. He already knew it and intended to make it right. He pushed his way to the front. "I'll pay for everyone's breakfast to make up for last night." He counted heads then dropped the appropriate amount into Joanna's palm. It made a dent in his funds, but it couldn't be helped.

Joanna turned to the waiting men. "Is that acceptable?"

Seems they were agreeable, and they trooped inside.

Levi took the children in, well aware Emmy squirmed in discomfort. This arrangement wasn't going to work. He'd have to figure out something else.

The others left before Emmy finished. In fact, she didn't start eating until they departed.

Joanna stood in the kitchen doorway. "Levi, can we talk to you?"

He knew what she wanted. "I'm sorry about last night."

The three women faced him. Even Glory looked regretful. For one second only, he allowed himself to look into her pale brown eyes and believe he saw understanding.

Of course he did. For the children. And what more did he

want or expect? Nothing more. Nothing at all.

"I'm sorry," Joanna said, as the spokeswoman for the trio. "But if we let you stay here, we'll ruin our business."

"I know. I'll find something else."

"Where?" Mandy demanded. "I don't know of any empty place in town."

"Except—" Joanna turned to stare at Glory.

"Of course." Mandy gave Glory her attention as well.

"Your room behind the shop," they said in unison. "It's furnished and everything."

"No. It just wouldn't work."

"Why not?" Again the pair spoke at once.

"She's right," Levi said, but they didn't hear him. He did not intend to move into her shop. See her at work every day. Be aware of her comings and goings. Be tempted to watch her. Speak to her. Wonder if she would perhaps drop in for a cup of coffee and a visit. How could he keep his mind on his task under such circumstances? "She's right," he said again, louder, more insistent.

All three stared at him.

"She is not." Mandy seemed shocked he would agree.

"Yes, I am." Glory's expression was rife with anger. He'd agreed with her, hadn't he? No reason she should be upset about it.

Joanna looked from Glory to Levi and back again. "You two fighting about something?"

"No, ma'am." Levi was firm in his denial.

Joanna turned to Glory and waited for her answer. When it wasn't forthcoming, she planted her hands on her hips. "Don't tell me. You've done something so outrageous you offended him."

"I did not." She glowered at Levi.

He couldn't help but grin. No, she hadn't. But he had. He'd

kissed her. Told her he was sorry. But was he? Not completely.

Joanna saw his grin. "Something is going on between you two. I can tell."

Levi shrugged, and Glory glowered, but neither offered an explanation.

Joanna sighed. "If that's the way you're going to be. . . Then what are you going to do with the children?"

"I'm not sure. Nothing seems ideal. But then anything is better than sitting alone at the side of the road." The thought cheered him. "We'll manage."

Only one option presented himself. He'd throw himself and his charges on Mr. Phelps's mercy. His house was tiny, but they could squeeze in.

He gathered up the children and their belongings and headed out. He'd check on Widow Kish first.

As he approached the house, he saw the door open. But as he drew closer, he saw the door was not just open. It was missing. Something was wrong. "Stay here," he told the children and dropped to the ground to ease forward.

A big sign had been nailed to the side of the shack. No Trespassing. Who would want to trespass and who would care? But someone obviously did.

He stepped inside. "Mrs. Kish? Are you here?" The place felt as empty as a licked-out tin can, but he investigated every corner and searched the clearing around the shack. Nothing. Nobody. What happened to the widow? All sorts of scenes raced to his mind. Someone had hurt her. She'd fallen somewhere and hurt herself. But none explained the absence of her belongings. Had she suddenly decided to move? But she said she had no family.

He mounted his horse again and turned back to town.

"Where's the lady we was supposed to see?" Emmy demanded.

"She's gone."

"Where?"

"I don't know."

"You gonna find her?"

Jack spoke from behind Levi. "Emmy, you ask too many questions."

"Well, if he's gonna find our pa, maybe he can find the lady, too."

They turned off at Mr. Phelps's house.

"Who lives here?" Emmy asked.

"A friend of mine."

"Will I like him?" She twisted around to look at Levi, forcing him to grab the back of her dress to keep her from falling.

"She talks too much," Jack muttered.

"Do not."

"Yes, you do. Even Pa said so."

Emmy's face grew instantly sad, and tears filled her big eyes. "Is that why he left?"

Jack relented of his scolding. "'Course not, silly. He had something to do. Remember?"

Levi wanted to find their father and demand an explanation. Why would he leave his children even for a moment? But right now he had to do something to restore Emmy's cheerfulness. "Probably right now he's wishing he could hear your voice." And if he wasn't, the man didn't deserve to be a father. Forbidden, his thoughts went to Glory. Seems her father didn't deserve the privilege either.

He took the children with him to the door, knocked, and went inside at Mr. Phelps's call to enter. He went into the kitchen and blinked. Widow Kish sat across the table from Mr. Phelps, and they were both drinking tea.

"Join us," Mr. Phelps called. "Though the children will

have to share a chair."

Levi pulled out a chair for the children and sat on the fourth, all the while trying to make sense of this situation. He turned to the widow. "I was at your place. It looks deserted."

"It is. The man who owns the land came by yesterday and said I had one hour to vacate his property. And let me tell you, he wasn't prepared to listen to reason. So I gathered up my things under his eagle eye and marched out without so much as a backward look." She gave a laugh, half-bitter, half-grateful. "I stopped to say good-bye to Mr. Phelps."

"I said I could use a housekeeper if she was interested."

"So here I am."

"It's good to know you're safe and sound. I had all sorts of thoughts about what happened to you."

"I'm sure I shall enjoy it here. Like the good Lord says, 'The lines are fallen unto me in pleasant places.'"

"I'm most grateful to have someone care for my home," Mr. Phelps said. He cleared his throat and looked embarrassed. "We're hoping you'll agree to marry us."

Levi grinned. "It would be an honor." His first wedding in Bonners Ferry. "Why don't we meet at the lawyer's office in a couple of hours?" It was indeed good news. . .for the widow and lonely Mr. Phelps. But it left Levi with no place to shelter the children. There would not be room for them here now.

But—he cheered up—if the Lord could provide for a widow woman, He could certainly provide for two abandoned children.

They visited awhile then Levi headed back to town.

He slowed his horse as he neared Glory's shop. The door was open, a man and four horses in the pen. Glory glanced up from her work, saw him, and straightened to study him.

Her gaze darted to the children then back to him. Then she turned to her work.

But had he seen regret in her gaze? Was she thinking of the sparsely furnished room at the back of her shop? It sounded mighty appealing just now. But he knew what would happen to his vow of service if he moved into it. He would not be able to keep his thoughts focused on working for the Lord. He'd think far too much about how he could show he cared for Glory.

Because, despite taking the words back, he cared.

And it could not be. He thought of Matt the last time he'd seen him, in leg irons and chains, a mask of toughness almost hiding the hurt and fear beneath. Perhaps only Levi saw it, but it was enough to convince him to help his brother. And he knew how. Serve God wholly and exclusively. Trust God to soften Matt's heart.

He hadn't changed his mind.

He rode on. Unless something else turned up in the next few hours, he would be making camp for the three of them among the trees. In fact there was no point in delaying the inevitable. First, he needed to meet Mr. Phelps and Widow Kish at the lawyer's office.

A little later, having duly married them, he headed for the store and some much-needed food supplies. Then he followed a little trail leading up the hillside.

"Where we going?" Emmy demanded.

"Would you like a picnic?"

"Yes."

He found a grassy clearing large enough to allow the sun to warm the air early in the morning. Trees surrounded them at a distance, and the blue mountains filled the horizon. "This will do." He set the children on the ground.

Free from the presence of strangers, Emmy let out a deep

sigh and with a shriek of delight started to run around the clearing.

Jack started after her then grew serious. "She's just little." He turned, somewhat reluctantly Levi thought, and reached out to take the gunnysack as Levi removed it from the back of the horse.

"I'm going to need some help building a shelter."

"This isn't just a picnic, is it?"

"It's where we'll sleep until I find something else."

"Or find our pa."

"I'll get at that right away." He would give the ferry man a message to hand off to someone he considered trustworthy enough to deliver to the North-West Mounted Police across the border.

He cut branches, and Jack helped him fashion a shelter. They found more branches to create a bed for them. The nights would cool off, but with a fire in front of the open side, they should be fine. And if it rained? Well. . .he hung a roll of canvas on the open side just in case.

He wasn't much of a cook, but they enjoyed pieces of cheese and biscuits, both of which he'd been able to purchase at the store. They remained there all afternoon, the children playing so happily he couldn't bear to take them away to return to town and check on. . .things. Mostly he thought of Glory and warned himself to remember his vow. Later, he fried up some salt pork for supper. If he felt comfortable leaving the children, he'd hunt some fresh meat. But he was reluctant to leave them.

The next morning, they had more biscuits and some canned peaches. The children ate heartily without complaint.

"I need to do some things today," he informed them after they'd eaten and cleaned up. "You'll have to come with me."

Emmy stuck out her chin, prepared to argue.

Jack grabbed her hand. "Come on."

"I don't want to. I'm having fun."

Jack faced her and grew very serious. "Emmy, you must not make him regret taking care of us."

"We was doing fine by ourselves, weren't we?"

"You were scared."

"Only at night."

"And when you saw people coming."

Her bottom lip quivered. "I was only hoping it was Pa."

Levi decided it was time to intervene and clear up any fears triggered by the suggestion Jack had made. "I'll never regret helping you two, but I need to send a message about your pa. You want to come with me?"

That brought an eager response from them both.

Their first stop was the ferry where Levi wrote the message on a piece of paper. The ferry man promised to see it into safe hands.

eight

For two days Glory watched Levi ride through town with the children. If she thought it would make him change his mind, she would track him down and insist he move into the little room adjoining her shop. It galled her to think of the children camping out, though they no doubt considered it an adventure.

Joanna had learned they had a rough camp up the hill. "That's no place to have children. Glory, you should persuade Levi to move into your room."

"You heard him. He doesn't want to." She managed to keep the bitterness from her voice. He made it clear he regretted stealing a kiss, saying he cared. Even living in a room she owned was too much. As if he couldn't abide a hint of her presence.

"Did you two argue about something? Did he say something when he stopped your horses?"

Joanna could be so dense sometimes.

"Of course he said something. Told me I was foolish."

Joanna chuckled. "You're certainly foolhardy. Even you can't deny that."

"I don't care what anyone thinks."

"Exactly. And Levi is a preacher. I expect he does care what people think. He must be circumspect."

"Or real good at fooling people."

Joanna jerked about to face her. "Glory, you don't believe that." Her eyes narrowed. "I suppose you accused Levi of being false. No wonder he avoids you."

"Does he? I hadn't noticed." She stomped away to take

care of her chores. Not for anything would she let Joanna guess how much it stung to realize even her sister was aware of Levi's attempt to stay as far away from her as possible. "I don't care." She said the words time and again but couldn't force herself to believe them.

Truth was, the dining room table seemed empty without him. The breakfast table lacked something.

She sat beside Toby now to peel potatoes and turnips.

"Levi said he's trying to find the children's father," Toby said. "Sent a message up north. Hopes he'll hear something soon."

Glory grunted acknowledgment of his statement.

"He says the children keep asking after their pa. They're afraid he won't know where to find them."

"Any father who cares wouldn't have left them in the first place."

"Levi says they had been traveling with some others and parted ways. Then their father realized his friend had left behind a sack of things. He had to ride hard to catch up and told the kids to wait for him. Said he'd only be half an hour or so."

"Long half hour."

"Levi says something must have happened."

Levi said. She didn't want to hear it again. Why did everyone else champion him while she felt dismissed, invisible? She hated the feeling. Hated that she couldn't control it.

"I've got something to do." She hurried to her shop, saddled Pal, and headed for the pen where her other horses looked up, anxious for their oats.

She had noticed the No Trespassing sign on Widow Kish's shack. No doubt put there by the same man who threatened to kick her and the horses off his land. Sure he had the right. But she didn't want to move. This was convenient. Had good grass and a beautiful view. But she didn't have enough money to purchase it.

And little faith God would help her.

She had barely arrived at the pen when it started to rain. She hadn't given the weather any thought and glanced around. The sky was heavy, threatening a downpour. Meant soggy wet clothes and muddy shoes around the table tonight. The air would be heavy with the smell of wet leather and damp wool.

But it wasn't the stopping house that was utmost in her mind. . . Levi and the children were camped out. According to both Toby and Joanna he had only a rough shelter. It would not be waterproof. The three of them would be cold and wet.

They'd be okay. She said the words over and over as if by repetition she could convince herself. But her efforts proved futile.

She pulled her slicker from where she kept it tied to the saddle, slipped it on, and headed back to town. Rain came down in sheets. It dripped from her hat brim, slashed against her face, drizzled down her neck. Spring rains could be awfully cold. Her hands were like winter ice, her legs as cold as yesterday's coffee.

Her thoughts had gone to a defenseless little girl. A boy who, no matter how miserable he felt, would not complain. And Levi's concern at knowing both children were suffering from the cold and wet. He wouldn't take them to the stopping house because of Emmy's fear of strangers, but there was one place where they could find protection from the elements and privacy from strangers. The room at the back of her shop. It was a perfectly good room. Seemed a shame for it to be empty. No need for them to get in each other's way.

She stopped at the house and stood in the doorway. "Jo," she yelled, not wanting to take off her wet things to go inside.

Joanna stuck her head from the kitchen. "What?"

"It's raining."

Joanna shook her head. "I know. Is that all you want?"

Glory hesitated. She wanted to let Joanna know where she was going. But she wanted more. Perhaps assurance she wasn't being a fool. "I expect the children will be wet and miserable."

"What children?" She leaned against the door and grinned. "Oh. You mean *Levi* and the children."

Glory wrinkled her nose at the way Joanna emphasized the word *Levi*. As if it had special importance. But she decided not to defend herself at the moment. "I'm going to persuade them to use the room at the shop. At least it's dry."

"About time you came to your senses."

"What's that supposed to mean?"

"If you can't figure it out yourself, I'm not going to waste my breath explaining. Go on. Get out of here."

As Glory turned to leave, Joanna called, "I'll send Mandy to fill the wood box and take up some things you'll be needing."

It wasn't until Glory rode from the yard she realized Joanna had said "you," as if taking for granted Glory would help Levi care for the children.

"About time," she'd said. "Figure it out yourself."

Glory grinned. She had it figured out already. She intended to make Levi take back his words about not being able to care. She pretended it was only out of spite, because it had hurt to have him take it back, but it was more than that. She wanted him to care about her.

She needed him to, even though she wanted it to be

otherwise. She was more than half certain she would regret cracking open a long shut door in her heart.

The trail to the ferry had turned into mud. She slogged through it and turned off at a narrow path. It, too, was slippery with mud. She spoke reassuringly to Pal. At least there was still light to pick her way cautiously.

A few minutes later she broke into a clearing. Immediately she saw a shelter made out of branches with a piece of canvas over the open side. The wind battered it, allowing rain to blow in at the ends. A campfire sputtered, sending out nothing but dank smoke. They would be cold and wet.

The damp grass muffled her approach. She reined in before the flapping canvas. "Hello. Anyone home?"

A faint sound came from behind the canvas.

She called out again, louder this time. "It's raining, in case anyone cares to notice."

"We noticed." Levi lifted the corner of the canvas. "You rode out here to tell us that?"

She studied him. His hat was off, his hair darkened by dampness. A poncho draped over his shoulders. "Where are the children?"

"In here." Jack's voice seemed to come from under Levi's arm.

"We're trying to keep dry." Emmy's voice came from under his chin.

"And are you? Keeping dry."

"No," Emmy said. "I'm cold, too."

"It seems a shame to sit out here and suffer when there's a dry, warm room back in Bonners Ferry."

Jack's face appeared beside Levi's. "There is?"

"Yup. Back room of my shop is empty. And I'm pretty sure there's a stove belching out heat right now."

Jack turned to Levi, his eyes wide with longing. "Emmy's awfully cold."

Glory guessed she wasn't the only one. The three of them looked like they'd been plucked from the river and left to drip in a brisk wind. She didn't feel much better herself, and the idea of a warm, dry room made her want to ride back to town without pause. But she couldn't leave the children to suffer any more than she could look at the discouragement in Levi's expression and not do something about it. "If you hand Emmy up to me, I'll tuck her under my poncho and take her to that room. You and Jack can follow."

Levi hesitated about one second then whipped his poncho off and wrapped it around Emmy, handing the child up to Glory.

"You have no protection." She saw the argument in his eyes. He'd suffer for the sake of the little girl. "Jack should be protected." She edged Emmy under her slicker and handed Levi's back. "Now let's get into some decent shelter." She didn't wait for Levi to call Billy Bob. Didn't linger to see if he and Jack would follow. She knew Levi could manage. Glory's greater concern was getting Emmy into a warm, dry place. The child was like a block of ice in her arms.

Pal fought for footing on the slippery trail.

"Be careful," Levi called from behind her.

"Always am." But it took a great deal of effort to hold Emmy close and guide Pal. She knew it would have been harder if she'd been on a horse with less common sense.

They reached the main trail, now a sea of mud, and sloshed through it to the shop. She'd left the gate open and rode straight in, Levi right behind. She didn't stop to take care of Pal or even close the gate but slid from the saddle with Emmy in her arms and raced into the room. The heat from the stove welcomed her.

Levi carried Jack inside and stood him on the floor.

A stack of towels and bedding waited on the bed. Joanna

must have sent them with Mandy.

"Take Jack through to the shop." She handed him a towel and indicated the door. "Strip his wet things off and rub him dry."

"What will I wear?" Jack clutched at his wet shirt, not wanting to be seen naked.

"We'll have to dry your clothes. In the meantime, wrap up in this." She tossed Levi a blanket. "Now get so I can take care of Emmy." Already she had begun to peel off the child's wet garments.

Emmy's eyes were big and as full of misery as an old hound dog's. She shivered and her teeth chattered enough to keep her from talking.

"You'll soon be warm." Glory tossed her wet things to one side to hang later and scrubbed Emmy dry, rubbing her hard to get her blood flowing. They stood inches from the stove. . . close enough that Glory's own damp clothes steamed.

She expected Emmy to stop shivering, but the child continued to quake. "Let's wrap you up in this blanket." She bundled up the child and drew a chair close, holding Emmy as close to the stove as she could stand. Still she shook. Glory held her tight and hummed softly, thinking she only needed to calm down. She should have insisted they use her room before this, but she'd let her pride get in the way.

Jack and Levi returned. Jack's color was good. He sat cross-legged on the floor, two feet from the stove. He let the blanket drape from his shoulders. Obviously he was warmed.

Levi knelt at Glory's side. "You still cold, little one?"

Emmy nodded, her eyes wide.

Levi turned his gaze toward Glory. "I shouldn't have been so stubborn."

"Me either."

Emmy continued to shiver.

They silently shared their concern. "Maybe a hot drink would help?"

Glory nodded. "I see Mandy left water and some supplies. Knowing Joanna there's likely tea and sugar there."

Levi hustled about filling the kettle and finding tea and sugar, but his gaze darted to Emmy every few seconds and then connected with Glory's eyes.

She tried not to watch his every move or admire the efficient way he did everything. Told herself his worry about Emmy was natural and normal. Nothing to make her insides feel empty. And when he looked into her eyes, silently letting her see his concern, there was no reason it felt like a warm, sweet drink. Except it did, and even though she told her brain not to read so much into it, her heart stubbornly followed its own way.

He poured hot water over the tea leaves and stood waiting for the tea to steep.

"Doesn't have to be too strong for her," Glory said after a moment.

He jolted like his thoughts were elsewhere. "Of course." He poured tea into a cup and ladled in a heaping spoonful of sugar. Tested the temperature of the liquid and grimaced. "Too hot." He added a bit of cold water, tested it again, and then satisfied he brought it over. He again squatted at Glory's side and held the cup to Emmy's mouth. "Drink some, sweetie. It will make you feel better."

He bent close to Emmy, giving Glory plenty of opportunity to study his profile. Strong-jawed as she already knew. Little contrasting lines fanning from the corner of his eyes from squinting into the harsh sunlight. An outdoor man. A tiny doubt niggled. Wasn't a preacher an inside sort of man? The thought barely had time to surface before she continued her study. Long, dark eyelashes. His hair was almost dry, thick and untamed. Like Levi himself. He didn't let Bull stop him from going into the saloon. He stood up to Glory even in her most angry defiance. Even said he cared. Though he'd taken it back.

Levi glanced up, caught her studying him, and sat back on his heels to match her look for look. Neither of them spoke. The only sounds were the crackle of wood in the stove, Jack's low murmur as he played with a bit of leather he'd found in the shop, and the chatter of Emmy's teeth.

It was the latter sound that made Glory blink and turn her attention to the child. "Aren't you getting warm yet?"

"My stomach is cold."

Levi looked startled. "That doesn't sound very good."

Glory wished she could say it was okay, but she didn't know. "All I know is to give her warm drinks and keep her wrapped warmly. Sooner or later she'll start to get warm." *Don't you think?* she silently asked Levi. Too bad there wasn't a doctor nearby.

He lifted one shoulder to indicate he didn't know. "Seems you're doing all that can be done." He urged Emmy to swallow the rest of the tea. He straightened, walked to the door, and stared at it then strode back to her side. "I should have found better shelter for them before this happened."

"How were you supposed to know it would rain?"

"Children deserve to be in the care of adults who know how to provide for them."

She held his gaze, seeing his frustration, understanding his feelings of inadequacy. Her own thought echoed his words. "Children need people to care for them." She'd let her feelings toward Levi make her neglectful of these children.

His eyes narrowed as if he thought she accused him of not caring. "I care about them. And even though I might have given you cause to think otherwise, I care about you."

Despite the shivering child in her arms, Levi's words warmed her. She ducked her head lest he see how pleased she was and delivered a firm warning to her heart. Likely by tomorrow he would be taking the words back again.

She continued to hold the child. Levi hovered at her side, touching Emmy's head every few minutes as if to check to see if she still shivered though one only had to look to see it.

His hand brushed Glory's shoulder as he reached for Emmy yet again. The nerves in her skin lit like a streak of lightning. She half-expected Emmy to jump from her lap, complaining she was too hot. But Emmy continued to shiver, and Glory knew the heat came from her own reaction. Levi was so close, his presence so overwhelming.

He crossed the room again, spun around, and hurried back. As if afraid to take his gaze from Emmy, as if unable to stand by and helplessly do nothing as she continued to shiver.

Glory wanted to ease his mind. "I'm sure she'll warm up soon. Won't you, Emmy?"

Emmy nodded without speaking, her eyes even wider than before if such a thing was possible.

"In fact, I think she's shivering less now."

Levi rushed to her side and dropped to a squat. He cupped the child's head in his hands and looked at her face, taking in each feature.

Glory wanted to close her eyes at the tenderness in Levi's gaze, but she couldn't deny herself one bit of it. Maybe Mandy was right. Maybe Glory was a tiny bit jealous of the attention he gave these children. Attention she'd never had from her father.

But it wasn't fatherly attention she longed for from Levi. She wanted him to see her as a woman with—

She daren't think of what she wanted. She had other things to occupy her time and thoughts. Like getting Emmy warmed. Like earning enough money to buy that piece of land. Like—

Levi pulled the covers tighter around Emmy, his knuckles grazing Glory's arm.

She suddenly couldn't remember anything more important than this moment and sharing it with Levi.

"She's still shivering."

She ducked her head and cradled the child close.

Levi paced the room, pausing at each passing to touch Emmy's head.

His restlessness scraped along her mind. She glanced at Jack. He had fallen asleep on the floor. "Best put him on the bed."

Levi scooped up the boy and laid him on the bed, covering him with the blanket, tucking it around him tightly as she'd noticed him do before.

Again, she ached deep inside for such comfort.

Levi pulled a chair up beside Glory. "Do you want me to take her?"

"She's fine here." Glory needed to hold the little girl. Needed something in her arms. Needed the weight of her body against her chest. She felt so empy inside, Levi's voice reverberating back and forth from one side of her rib cage to the other. She had to find a way to put this agony to an end. "How did your parents die?"

"Influenza."

"And you and your brother didn't get sick?"

"No. Thank the good Lord."

"Where's your brother now?"

For a moment he didn't answer, and Glory shifted so she could watch his expression. Pain flickered through his eyes, and she wondered at the cause. Then his eyes hardened. "He's away. He'll be gone for some time."

A traveler then. "I suppose you miss him."

"A lot."

She shifted to a more comfortable position. "I always wished I had a brother. What's it like?"

He laughed softly. "Sort of like having you for a sister, I expect."

"What's that supposed to mean?" She gave him a hard look, prepared to defend herself.

"Don't get all prickly on me. But I've seen you and your sisters teasing each other and laughing at shared jokes. And"—his eyes darkened with their own teasing—"I've seen you angry enough at Mandy to try and chase her down. I expect you wanted to tie a lickin' on her."

She drew her chin up and gave him a dismissive look. "I would never beat her up."

His laughter deepened, sending ripples through her insides. "If that's true, I would venture to guess it's only for two reasons."

She wouldn't give him the satisfaction of asking what they were. She wouldn't. Un-uh. But the words burst from her mouth. "What two reasons?"

His satisfied grin notified her he had been aware of her futile mental struggle. "First, you couldn't catch her, and second, if you did try, Joanna would separate the two of you."

She sniffed. No way would she admit he was correct. Never.

He chuckled softly, a sound as full and rich as thick, sweet chocolate. "I see I'm right."

"You see nothing."

"You're wrong there. I see a lot of things."

Dare she challenge him? No. She wouldn't. She wouldn't invite him to make observations. But she couldn't let it be. "What things do you see about me?"

He shifted to face her, his gaze exploring her chin, skimming her cheeks, coming to rest on her eyes. Indeed, he seemed to see way deeper than what most people saw. His look probed the secret places of her heart.

She held her breath as he contined to study her.

"I see a beautiful woman who is as prickly as a pincushion. And as cautious and fearful as a trapped fawn."

She swallowed hard, unfamiliar emotions clogging her throat.

He touched her cheek, brushed aside a strand of hair she hadn't been aware of. "I see a woman who is afraid to let herself feel. She's afraid to be real, let her feelings have expression because she's so often been disappointed and hurt."

She wanted to narrow her eyes, deny his words, laugh them off as false, but she couldn't. No more than she could pull back from his probing, owning look.

He sighed and sat back, freeing her from his scrutiny. "Unfortunately I fear I will only add to your hurt."

"Excuse me?" What on earth did he mean?

"Yes. You see, I care about you. Far more than I have a right. I think you might end up hurt and disappointed."

"Really." She put as much sarcasm into the word as she could muster, but it still sounded far too begging for her liking.

"Yes. You see, I have a purpose that leaves me no room for anything else."

He as much as admitted he wasn't a preacher like he said. She tried to put that thought on top of her confusion, but it sank, leaving her staring at the things he'd said about her. He understood her as no one else did, not even her sisters. Why couldn't he simply be her friend and maybe more? She licked her lips and forced her wooden tongue to work. "A man can always change who he is and what he does."

For a moment he didn't answer. She held her breath hoping he would agree. Instead he shook his head. "Not always, I'm afraid." He planted his palms on his knees and slowly pushed to his feet. "How's she doing?"

"She's quit shivering. In fact, she must be getting hot." She folded back the blanket. "She's flushed." She lowered the woolen cover. "She's burning up." The child was naked. Glory grabbed a towel to cover her. She saw an old nightie Joanna must have stuck in and pulled it over Emmy's head. "Do you suppose she's taken a chill?"

"I don't know. What do we do?"

She'd never nursed a child. Only animals. She tried to calm her thoughts and think how to handle this situation.

The door crashed open, and Mandy strode in with more wood. "Joanna sent me to see if you were okay. You've been gone a long time. I took care of the horses."

Glory and Levi exchanged guilty looks. They'd forgotten the horses. For the first time she could remember, Glory had neglected an animal.

Mandy took in the pair of them huddled over Emmy.

Glory groaned. No doubt Mandy would read a lot more into the scene than it deserved. "I think Emmy's sick."

Mandy dropped the wood in the box and crossed to Levi's side. "How do you know?"

"She's so hot."

"Well, it is like a furnace in here." Mandy cracked open a window.

Levi scooped Emmy from Glory's arms and took her to the bed. She opened her eyes at the disturbance.

Jack groaned and rolled toward the wall.

"Don't her eyes look glassy?" Glory asked.

The three adults stood gazing at her.

"You ever been sick?" Glory asked Levi, hoping he might

have some personal experience with this sort of thing.

"Wouldn't dare."

"What's that supposed to mean?"

"My grandparents thought it a sign of weakness. Before that I only remember my ma giving me sweet licorice tea if I didn't feel well. You?"

"Never had time for it." And hadn't paid much attention when she'd seen little ones ill. Glory turned to Mandy. "You once had the measles. Ma made you stay in bed in a dark room and insisted you drink lots of water." She bent close to Emmy. "Would you like some water?"

Emmy groaned and turned her head away.

"I don't suppose that's a good sign," Levi said.

"What do we do?" Glory looked from Mandy to Levi, wanting an answer.

They both shook their heads.

She faced Levi. "You say you're a preacher. Shouldn't you know how to help people?"

He lifted his hands in a helpless gesture. "I've never been responsible for someone so young."

"What are we going to do?" Glory didn't know if she was more scared or more angry that none of them knew. "I don't know if we should wrap her up and keep her warm or uncover her and cool her off, but there's one person who will know. Joanna. Mandy, run and ask her what we should do."

Mandy was gone before Glory finished speaking.

Suddenly she noticed how Emmy's breath whistled in and out. She turned to Levi. "Is she going to be alright?"

Levi reached for Glory's hands. "We're going to do all we can."

She sought and found comfort in his eyes, in his promise, and in the strength of his grip.

nine

Levi held Glory's hands and looked deep into her eyes—almost golden in the last of the watery daylight. Apart from worry about Emmy, he had enjoyed the afternoon with her. He'd likely not get another and would forever cherish the few hours they'd been able to spend together in harmony.

When she rode into the wet campsite, he'd never heard a more welcome voice. For the sake of the children he went with her, though it wasn't hard to make the choice. Yes, he knew he couldn't offer her anything more than an afternoon or maybe two. Maybe three or four.

He stopped right there. No more counting. No more giving himself excuses. Or reasons. He'd been as honest with her as he could be, but still, he had no intention of hurting her.

Her eyes filled with worry and—dare he think it?—trust. Just a hint of such. He gripped her hands harder, vowing he would do all he could to deserve that trust. Which meant not caring for her, not allowing her to care for him.

For two heartbeats he considered changing his mind about devoting his life to serving God. But recalling the misery in Matt's expression and knowing nothing would change unless Matt's heart changed, Levi knew he must keep his bargain with God. At whatever cost.

"Is she going to be okay?" Glory demanded again.

"I am at a loss to know what we can do except for one thing and perhaps the best thing. Pray."

She sucked in a sharp breath. "Of course. I keep telling

God I am going to trust Him more. Believe His promises and all that sort of stuff. Then I forget." Her grin was crooked, her expression regretful.

"He understands our humanness and doesn't judge us for it. All He asks is that we turn back to Him after every lapse."

"Sounds awfully forgiving."

"Always. After all, God loved us enough, was forgiving enough to pour the punishment we deserved on His sinless Son."

She swallowed hard. "Makes me think how much I owe Him. A debt I can never repay."

"But that's the wonder of it. God doesn't expect us to try and pay it back. It would be impossible. God's love and forgiveness are gifts." Something about what she said tugged at his thoughts. As if he missed some detail, overlooked an important connection. But he couldn't find the elusive thing and let it go. This was not the time to explore his own problems.

He shifted his hands and held both of Glory's in one and rested the other on her shoulder, feeling her quiver beneath his touch and then calm as she drew in a deep breath. "Shall we pray?" It took every ounce of self-control to remember his responsibility here—to act like a preacher—when his heart called out for him to pull her into his arms, press her to his chest, comfort and hold her. He stiffened his arm and bowed his head. "Lord God, the One who loves us, touch little Emmy's hot body and cool it. Help no harm come to her. Amen."

He kept his eyes closed and silently prayed for strength and self-control to keep his eyes on the task set before him, the road he had chosen. He needed it as never before as Glory leaned into his touch.

Time to shift things before he couldn't control his emotions.

He withdrew his hand from her shoulder but continued to clasp her hands. "Tell me how you came to be a farrier."

She blinked, obviously startled by his sudden shift of focus.

He grinned. "I'm only trying to get us thinking of something else. Maybe ease our worry."

"Isn't prayer supposed to do that?"

"I simply thought it would help the process."

She studied him a full ten seconds until he wanted to squirm.

"Stop looking at me like that. It reminds me of my grandmother."

Glory blinked then patted her face. "I've got wrinkles?"

His chuckle came from deep inside, a place where he stored secret pleasures. "Not wrinkles. Just a way of looking at me that makes me think you can read my mind."

"Maybe I can." She looked mysterious as if trying to convince him she saw many secrets.

He met her look without flinching, not caring if she saw secrets. He longed to open his heart to her and share the hidden contents with her. But he had made a vow, and God did not look kindly upon people breaking vows made to Him.

"How did you become a preacher?" she asked, her quiet voice pulling him from his mental wandering.

"I'll tell you if you answer my question first."

"What question would that be?" Her look of confusion didn't convince him she'd forgotten, and he only grinned for answer.

"Very well. When I was about thirteen, our pa left us with a couple who ran a livery barn. We were expected to work to earn our keep. So I learned to look after the horses and bothered the man to teach me how to trim hooves and shoe the horses. He might never have done so except one day he cut his hand badly and needed my help."

"I'm sure he never regretted it."

She lifted one shoulder in a gesture of uncertainty and indifference. "Couldn't say. Pa showed up shortly after that and dragged us off to another place. Where he promptly left us high and dry again. This time we refused to live with the family he'd stuck us with. One thing about having to work for our keep, we'd learned lots of things, so we started working for ourselves."

"You did farrier work?"

"Or whatever would bring in a few coins. Like train horses who had been ruined by mistreatment."

"That blue roan wouldn't be one of them, I suppose?"

"Yup. Pal, too. Horses can develop some very bad habits."

"Just like people." They searched each other's eyes. He found himself going deep, into her hurt. "You rescue hurt horses because they remind you of yourself."

Shutters blocked her feelings. Her eyes darkened. "It's your turn."

"Actually, becoming a preacher was almost natural. My grandfather was one. Several times as he grew older and was too weak to stand behind the pulpit, he asked me to do it. I guess you could say I inherited the job."

"I expect you had a choice in the matter."

"Don't we always?" Matt had the same choices as Levi and had chosen the opposite.

Again, he and Glory looked at each other. Studied each other. Her brown eyes revealed wonder at his question as if the idea of a choice was new to her. "Most times our choices are driven by what others choose to do."

He struggled to pull himself back from the pain and anger in her voice and in her eyes. If he didn't step away mentally, he would pull her into his arms and hold her tight, promise he would never do anything to hurt her, always protect her.

"Others do things that impact our lives. . .sometimes in a cruel way." *Lord, keep me from hurting Glory.* "Seems to me we still have a choice about whether to let it make us bitter or whether to rise above it."

She sucked in air hard. Blinked. Again shuttered her emotions. "Maybe so."

The door banged open, sending a rush of cold, damp air across the room.

Glory sprang away from him, clutching her hands to her waist.

Joanna strode in, Mandy at her heels. "I hear the little one is sick."

Glory nodded. "Burning up. I didn't know what to do." She tossed a glance over her shoulder at Levi. "None of us did."

Did he detect regret in her gaze? Was it regret at their discussion being interrupted? Or regret at the choices flung into her life by others? He hoped it was a tiny bit of the former, even though he knew he must guard his feelings very carefully.

Joanna leaned over the child, pressed her hand to Emmy's forehead.

Emmy stirred and moaned.

"Get me a basin of lukewarm water."

Mandy hurried to do so.

"And a washcloth."

Glory plucked one from the pile.

"You have to get the fever to break. Sponging her to cool her body is the only way I know." She pushed the baggy nightgown out of the way and set to washing Emmy's chest and legs, letting her skin dry in the warm air.

The adults hovered at the side of the bed as Joanna sponged Emmy over and over.

Thankfully, Jack crowded to the far edge of the bed and

turned his back toward them, able to sleep through the disturbance.

Time ceased to exist for those watching Joanna work and waiting for her to declare Emmy was going to be okay.

Twice, Glory looked at Levi, her eyes wide with appeal. He nodded. And at her silent urging, prayed aloud for the fever to leave.

Suddenly Mandy straightened. "It's stopped raining."

They glanced at the window. Saw it was dark outside.

Joanna paused from her task. "Mandy, you'll have to go back to the stopping house so people can bed down."

Mandy hesitated.

"I'll let you know as soon as Emmy is okay."

"You won't forget?"

Joanna spared her a quick look. "I won't forget."

Mandy slipped away.

"I can take over," Glory said and edged Joanna aside. "You sit down for a while."

Joanna looked about ready to argue.

"I'll make tea," Levi offered.

"Has anyone eaten?" Joanna, always concerned about caring for everyone.

Glory's attention was on the child, which left Levi to answer Joanna. "We haven't had time."

Levi made tea and poured Joanna a cupful where she sat at the table. He offered to take Glory's place so she could sit with her sister.

"I need to do this."

Levi sat across from Joanna. Need? Why did she say it that way? As if it was her responsibility.

Joanna sipped her tea. "She can't stand to see any living thing suffer without doing something."

"She told me about the horses."

"I tell her she's taking care of her own hurts by helping them."

Levi chuckled. "I said something similar."

He and Joanna smiled silent understanding at each other.

"I'm right here," Glory groused. "I can hear every word you say."

Joanna and Levi grinned at each other. He couldn't speak for Joanna, but he'd wanted Glory to hear every word.

Glory sat back on her heels and released a gust over her teeth. "I don't think she's so hot anymore."

Joanna sprang to her side, ran her hands over Emmy's body. "Her fever has broken. Thank You, God."

"Amen," Glory and Levi chorused and grinned at each other in shared joy.

Joanna pulled a sheet over Emmy. "She'll have to be watched carefully to make sure the fever doesn't return."

"I'll watch her," Glory said.

Joanna studied Glory. Levi wondered if she would tell Glory it was inappropriate to stay here with him after dark.

Glory must have expected the same thing. "I can't leave until I'm sure she's okay."

Joanna nodded. "I know. I understand. But I must get back to the stopping house." She hesitated. "I'll send Mandy back with supper. She can stay with you." She hesitated and looked as if she wanted to say more then shook her head and ducked out the door.

Glory straigthened and met Levi's look. The air between them grew still as if neither breathed.

He couldn't say what she was thinking, but for himself he felt as if they shared a special moment, a special awareness of each other, of having shared a common concern and conquered it. He shifted his gaze to Emmy—their common concern. She lay peaceful, her color normal.

He brought his eyes back to Glory. She watched him, waiting.

He closed the distance between them until they were only inches apart. Everything in him wanted to pull her into his arms and hold her close. Let his heart thud against his chest in acceptance of his feelings. He reached out and caught a strand of hair from off her cheek. Silky. He curled it around his finger and tugged at it. Strong. Just like Glory. Tough and resilient. Yet fragile. She'd been hurt in the past, and if he wasn't careful he could very well hurt her yet again.

Sucking in every bit of self-control he could muster, he freed his finger from her hair and dropped his arm to his side. "Are you hungry?" A stupid question when his mind burgeoned with so many more demanding things, like what did she feel toward him?

"Now that you mention it, I suppose I am." She spun away and went to the table, gathering up the cups used when they had tea. "Mandy will be back soon with food."

Although he was hungry, he didn't care about food. So many things crowded his heart and mind. Things he couldn't voice. He forced forward the reminder of Matt in chains. Now in a tiny prison cell. Slowly, determinedly, he brought his vow into focus. For Matt, for his salvation, for his redemption, Levi would give up everything but service to God.

⁂

When Mandy returned, her arms full of food and other things Joanna thought they might need, Glory let herself draw in the first full breath she'd taken since Joanna left.

Why did Levi touch her and then pull back? Not that it mattered to her. It was strange, that was all. Reminded her of Big Gray, the gelding who shivered when she touched him.

Had Levi been hurt by something? That piqued her curiosity.

Mandy put a pot of stew on the stove and a plate of biscuits on the table. She lifted the lid off the pot and sniffed. "I'm hungry."

The aroma of the stew filled the room, and Glory realized she was, too.

Jack sat up. "Is that food?"

Glory stared at the boy. Startled, she turned toward Levi and saw a matching expression.

Levi blinked. "Nothing will disturb that boy's sleep but the smell of food." He held Glory's gaze as he laughed.

She laughed, too, her tension disappearing. She'd let her imagination and her innate wariness make her see things not there. Maybe she was the one like Big Gray.

The four of them sat at the tiny table, enjoying the food and laughing as Mandy told them of the near riot at the stopping house because the men had to wait while she prepared the room for sleeping.

Later, Jack crawled back into bed and fell asleep. Levi watched him in wonder. "You'd think he hadn't slept in days."

"When was the last time he slept in a bed?" Glory asked. "And apart from the unsettling night in the stopping house, when did he last sleep in a room with four walls? I'm guessing he feels safe for the first time in many a day."

Levi continued to study the sleeping Jack. "Trusting us to take care of him." He slowly faced Glory, a look of determination hardening his eyes.

She couldn't pull away from that look. Could not think what it meant.

Mandy yawned loudly. "I know how Jack feels. I just want to curl up somewhere and sleep."

Glory checked Emmy. "She's still okay. Sleeping like a baby. Perhaps we should waken her and give her some broth."

Levi sank to the edge of the bed and shook Emmy gently.

"Wake up, little one."

Emmy cracked open her eyes and allowed Levi to hold her upright while Glory spooned in the warm liquid. Soon her head lolled to one side, and Levi laid her down again.

Mandy grabbed a blanket and a pillow and settled in a corner. She was soon breathing deeply, though Glory knew she was a light sleeper. She would waken instantly and be completely alert if any sudden noise disturbed her.

She and Levi sat at the table. Glory tried to keep herself amused and her thoughts distracted by tracing the cracks on the tabletop.

"I had hoped to hear something about their father by now." Levi's voice was soft.

"It's hard to find a man who doesn't want to be found."

"I can't believe he would abandon the children at the side of the road. Not intentionally. Something must have happened."

A thousand arguments sprang to her mind. But obviously he didn't understand how leaving was easy for some people. That not everyone had someone to fall back on apart from brothers or sisters. And when they were as young as Jack and Emmy, that wasn't much more than comfort. "You must have been grateful your grandparents took you in when your parents died."

For a moment he didn't answer, and she studied him. What she saw was not gratitude but regret.

"I appreciated having a home, but they were very strict. Our parents had allowed us a lot more freedom than our grandparents were prepared to give us." He paused. "It was hard to adjust."

"But you did."

"I tried. It was harder for Matt. He was seventeen and thought he was an adult, had to answer to no one. The only reason he hung about was to make sure I would be okay. And then he left."

"Did you see him again?"

"Off and on."

The man must travel a lot. Not unlike Pa. And maybe for the same reasons, adventure but also escape from responsibility. "You miss him."

"Yes. I'll do anything to get him back."

"What can you do? Like you said, he's a man now. He makes his own choices."

"I'm trusting God to change him."

She studied that for a few minutes. "Does trusting come easy for you?"

A chuckle rumbled from his chest. "Not always. You work with mishandled horses, right?"

She nodded.

"How hard it is for them to learn to trust? And then how often and how quickly do they retreat if something frightens or threatens them?" He gave another deep-throated chuckle. "Guess I feel like one of those horses. I trust God, but every time something challenges it, I have to learn to trust all over."

"It's hard for a mistreated horse to learn to trust at all."

The way he looked at her, she knew he understood she wasn't talking solely about animals. "So what do you do?"

"I just keep proving they can trust me. I just keep being kind. Giving them oats. That sort of thing."

"Not unlike how God treats us."

She checked Emmy as she contemplated his words. Liked how they made her feel about God. "I'm trying to learn to trust." The child's skin felt a normal temperature, and she returned to her chair.

"Me, too."

As they sat in the yellow light, the quiet around them as

cozy as a blanket, it was easy to think of him as honest, a real preacher. She let herself be lulled by the atmosphere as they talked about things they did as children, about horses they had known, and various other topics. They took turns checking on Emmy and sighed with relief when her fever didn't return.

The sky lightened.

"It's morning." Levi sounded as surprised as she felt. It was impossible they had spent the whole night talking.

Glory stared out the window. Something had changed in her feelings toward him. She felt as if she had tasted the oats he'd offered. Wanted more. But she wasn't sure she even trusted him. Was he who and what he said he was? She tried to reconcile her doubts with the things she'd seen— his prayers, the way he took care of those in need, his own struggles with trust. . .

She didn't know what to believe.

Mandy tossed aside the blanket and scrambled to her feet. "Is little Emmy okay?"

"Slept all night. No fever."

"Good. Then if you and I know what's good for us, we better get back and help Joanna."

Glory needed no more excuse to head for the door. She barely glanced at Levi, not trusting herself to hide her confusion and uncertainty.

Outside, she and Mandy strolled toward the stopping house.

"I heard you and Levi talking all night." Mandy nudged Glory and giggled. "Seems you've changed your mind about the man."

"We were talking about horses. He knows a lot about horses for a preacher." She forced suspicion into her voice.

"Well, he rides. I would hope he knows something about

the animal under his saddle." She moved far enough away to be out of reach. "I heard you talking about trust. I guess you're learning how to trust a man instead of shoving him into a naughty corner along with Pa. Where, I might point out, he doesn't belong, just as lots of the men don't. I like Levi. He's a good man."

"You're so willing to trust every man that you scare me."

Mandy stopped and stared. "I am not."

"Always ready to give Pa an excuse for leaving."

Mandy snorted and stomped onward. "At least I don't run from every man like he was poison."

"I just find it hard to trust all the words that come from a man's mouth."

Mandy, several steps ahead, turned to face her. "Now there's a sudden revelation." She wrinkled her nose in mocking.

Glory laughed. "Guess I'm pretty obvious, aren't I?"

ten

Levi got the children up, helped them put on their clothes that had dried overnight, and made a simple breakfast from the supplies Joanna sent over. He'd make a point of going by later in the day and paying her for them. After watching Emmy carefully for an hour or more, he came to the conclusion she had recovered from her illness the night before.

What a night it had been. He'd cracked open his heart to Glory, tentatively sharing things with her, knowing he must maintain strict boundaries and yet finding such sweet solace in telling her of his childhood.

She told story after story of the horses she'd worked with—abused, mishandled, neglected. Levi wondered if she realized how much she revealed of herself when she told about earning an animal's trust, the way the animals tested her. He guessed she would have stopped talking if she had.

He watched Jack and Emmy play at the table. Seems they could amuse themselves quietly if they had to. Could he persuade someone else to watch them while he crossed the river to go look for their father? He knew one person he would trust to have consideration for their feelings—Glory. While he waited for her to open the shop, he tended to dishes, and generally made the place liveable. He heard her at the shop door. "Come on, kids. We're going out."

Jack dashed to the door as eager as a young kitten to be outside. Levi carried Emmy.

Already the sun had dried the tiny pasture next to the shop

where Billy Bob and Pal grazed. He edged around to the front of the shop.

Glory had stepped inside and didn't noticed his approach until his boots thumped on the step. She spun around, and when she saw it was him, her expression went from welcome to caution.

He had business to attend to. For a moment he diverted himself as he put Emmy on her feet. He focused on that in order not to think of the gentle hours of last night. He removed his hat and turned it 'round and 'round in his hands. "How much is the rent on this place?"

She hesitated. He could practically see her thoughts churning. "I'd let you stay for free, but I need money to buy more oats for my horses."

"I can afford it," Levi assured her. He had funds left from the amount he had set aside for living on. He didn't intend to dip into the money he'd earmarked for starting a permanent work here—money he'd use as he felt the Lord direct.

"Two dollars for the month."

"Two dollars?" he sputtered. "You sure?" It was far less than he knew she could reasonably ask.

"You ever known me to lie?"

He correctly read the challenge in her voice. "No, ma'am. Not once. Didn't mean to imply otherwise. Promise you won't challenge me to a shootout at high noon."

Glory rolled her eyes to let him know just what she thought of his foolishness, noticed the worried look on the children's faces, and leaned close to whisper, "He's just being silly."

Emmy shrugged one shoulder. "I knew that. Sort of."

Levi whispered to the children as well. "I was just being cautious. She's not the sort you want to fool around with."

Emmy giggled.

Jack took a minute to decide if they were joshing or serious, but when he saw the pleased look on Levi's face at making Emmy laugh, he chuckled.

Glory tossed her hands skyward and let out a groan. "I can see I'll get nothing but silliness from the three of you." But she grinned, ruffled Jack's hair, and squeezed Emmy's shoulder.

Levi met her look and held it. He didn't free her from his intensity as he leaned back on his heels and studied her.

She shifted her eyes past his shoulder, but her gaze returned as if she couldn't look away.

"This room will be just the place for us until I find their pa."

"Yup," she said. "Might teach you a few important lessons."

"Like what?" She sounded almighty pleased about something, and he suspected it wasn't about last night.

She half-turned away. "Things like nightmares, silly fears, foods that gag certain people, and. . .things like saying something then taking it back. You don't get to do that with kids."

So they were back to the start. He caught her shoulder and spun her about to face him. "Glory, I didn't mean to hurt you. I don't plan to hurt you again." Why then did he allow an evening of quiet talk, sharing memories and experiences, and why above all was he so stupidly happy to rent a room from her? A room sharing a wall with her business where she would show up every morning?

"I wasn't talking about me."

"Yes, I think you were." But he had already gone over the line and he must stop right there and retreat. He pulled two dollars from his pocket and handed it to her.

She hestiated as if reconsidering.

"Take it."

She grabbed the money and stuffed it in her pocket.

He grinned, knowing she fought a desire to tell him to pack his bags and leave. She might have except for the children. He didn't doubt she cared about them. She understood how it felt to be waiting for their pa, afraid, uncertain, and with no place to belong.

Just thinking of it made his insides twist like he'd swallowed a bitter drink. Though it was as much on Glory's behalf as the children's. "I need some help," he murmured.

Glory chuckled softly. "I'm sure you'll manage just fine, Mr. Preacher Man." She turned her back. "I need to attend to my chores."

She'd misunderstood him. Thought he meant with looking after the children. It was sort of what he meant, and he decided to push the idea and grabbed her arm. "Have mercy on three poor souls."

She froze in place, one hand extended toward her worktable, her head half-turned toward the window.

A snap of silent power blazed up his arm and pooled in his heart like he'd barely missed being struck by a bolt of lightning. He'd touched her before, several times last night, but this time was different. This time it was daylight. There was no crisis with the children to excuse his touch. He pulled back and forced his tone to remain teasing. "You wouldn't leave us to manage on our own, would you?"

The children watched in confusion.

Glory blinked, seemed to shake herself. Her gaze went only as far as the children, and she seemed to struggle to remember their presence. Then she grinned down at them. "Do you think he's being silly again?"

They nodded, still not quite sure what to make of it. Emmy looked up from under her thick eyelashes. "Maybe he could use some help. He can't cook."

Levi couldn't believe his ears. "I haven't let you starve."

Emmy sighed. "'Preciate your kindness and all, but I'm getting a mite tired of hard biscuits and jerky."

"Shush, Emmy," Jack warned.

Glory tipped her head back and laughed.

Levi shoved his hat back on his head to hide his confusion. He thought he was doing just fine at looking after the children even though he was admittedly inexperienced.

"Where's my pa? Why didn't he come back for us?" Emmy choked out the words.

He reached out to pull them close. "Something must have happened to detain him. I'm sure we'll hear from him soon. Likely he's on his way back for you right now."

Glory nudged him aside. "Don't make promises you can't keep or have to take back."

Her words stung. "I didn't."

"Yes, you did. You can't know if he'll come back or not."

Emmy wailed louder. "I want my pa."

Glory knelt before the pair. "I can't say what happened to your pa. Seems you'll have to wait and find out. But right now you have a safe, warm place to stay."

He was surprised she didn't tell them to buck up. Not that he had anything to offer them but words of assurance he based on nothing more than hope and goodwill.

Emmy scrubbed at her eyes with her fists. "How long has your pa been gone?" she asked Glory.

Glory's expression hardened. "He's been in and out of my life since I was Jack's age."

"Don't it bother you?"

Levi watched, wondering how she would answer. Would she admit it did, made her wary, defensive?

She leaned forward, bringing herself to eye level with the children. "I can't say it doesn't bother me, but that's just how it is. I can't change anything."

Emmy nodded. "I guess not." She sucked in air. "I'll be okay."

Glory lifted her face toward Levi, a look of admiration on her face at the child's sudden acceptance of the facts.

Levi wanted to protest. Do something to prove to them all they could trust a man. A father. He addressed Glory. "Tell you what. If you would watch the children for me, I'll go and find their pa."

Glory took two steps away and looked at Levi with eyes darkened with suspicion.

"I'll be back. I promise."

"How can I look after them? I've got my work." She waved an arm around the little shop. "My horses." A vague wave to indicate some place beyond town. "My chores at the stopping house."

"They're right here. You can keep an eye on them as you work. Take them with you the rest of the time. Just spend the night here so they aren't alone."

Two pairs of big brown eyes begged her to do it, far more effectively than any words he could utter.

She sighed. Gave him a look of warning.

He read her loud and clear. *You better not run out on this.*

"I'll be back unless I'm dead. You can count on it. In fact"—he opened the notebook she kept on her worktable, tore out a page, and wrote on it—"I will carry this in my pocket just in case." He handed the note to her.

She read aloud, her voice growing incredulous by the end. " 'In case of my demise, please return my body to Miss Glory Hamilton at Bonners Ferry. Inform her of the circumstances of my death and tell her I tried to get back.' It doesn't matter to me. I just don't want to see the children building false hope." With a flick of her wrist, she tossed the note at him.

He caught it and stuck it in his pocket.

She gave him a look fit to crispy-fry bacon. "I'll watch them. You go find a missing father."

"Which one. Theirs or yours?" He didn't know what possessed him to say such a thing, but now that he had, he waited to see her reaction.

She pulled the two children to her side. "I don't need a father. They do." Her eyes challenged him to think otherwise.

Wisely, he held his tongue, but as he crossed on the ferry, he prayed not only to find Mr. Templeton but also Mr. Hamilton. He'd demand both men return and face their children.

⋆

"If anyone can find Pa, Mr. Powers can," Emmy insisted as Glory prepared her for bed.

"I'm just saying don't get your hopes too high."

"Mr. Powers told us to pray. He said God listens to even little girls."

Glory closed her eyes for a moment. She used to believe it without question, but her prayers for her pa to come back and take care of them had never been truly answered. Now she was trying to learn to trust God all over. Right now her fervent prayer was for God to provide a way for her to buy the land where she was keeping her horses.

Jack sat on the edge of the bed, waiting for Glory to read them a story and tuck them in. "I remember Pa saying sometimes it's hard to trust when it seems things are going wrong, but that's when we need to trust the hardest."

Glory glanced at the boy. Where did such a young person get such wisdom? Did he suspect Levi would not return with the hoped-for, prayed-for result? Was he preparing himself for the worst? "Trust is indeed hardest when we need it worst." And when she needed it most she'd let it go. No more. Levi was right. God's promises weren't subject to change.

She tucked the children in and listened to their breathing grow deep as she sat at the table and read from the Bible. But her thoughts kept drifting. Would Levi be able to find their father? Would he happen to run into her pa, too? And if he did. . . ?

She would not allow herself any dreams or hopes. Instead, she prayed for Levi to find the children's father and bring him back to claim his children.

Two days later and she waited impatiently for the answer to two prayers—a way to buy the land and a man returning on a black horse with a second man at his side.

She sat helping Toby peel potatoes while Emmy and Jack perched a few yards away, watching the ferry.

All her old doubts and fears returned. Rawhide Kid disguising himself as a preacher. "Looking for someone has given him a handy excuse to disappear for a few days. Maybe I'll ask the ferry man to get someone to pick up a newspaper from up in the territories. Might provide interesting reading."

Toby grunted. "I think the man could live a pure life for ten years and you'd still be looking for signs of something unlawful. Maybe even that wouldn't be enough." He suddenly faced her, his expression half-mournful, half-accusing. "Glory, what would it take to make you trust a man?"

His question caught her off guard. She had to think about it. Finally, she realized she didn't have an answer. "Don't ever plan to need to trust a man." A tiny voice deep inside reminded her of how nice it had been to share those hours with Levi not so long ago. For a little while, she'd let herself forget her doubts and suspicions.

Only because Emmy's illness and the darkness had lulled her. It wouldn't happen again.

Emmy and Jack crossed the yard and stood before her. "Why hasn't Levi come back?" Emmy demanded, the momentary spokesman for the pair.

The question echoed inside Glory's head, reminding her of all the times she had asked the question about her pa. But she didn't want to be the one to shatter this pair's world. Life would surely do it soon enough. "He promised he'd come back, didn't he?" Dead or alive.

Toby snorted at how her words contradicted what she'd said only a moment before.

"You just have to be patient."

After supper, the children returned to their station, wanting to watch until the last ferry crossed.

Glory let them. After all, she had chores to do and wasn't anxious to be shut up in the tiny room, wondering and waiting.

Later, she returned to the room and put the children to bed. She was tired, but sleep did not come easily as her thoughts chased down blind trails. *What if he doesn't come back? What will happen to the children?* She'd make sure they were safe. Joanna and Mandy would surely welcome them to stay at the stopping house. Emmy would get used to all the people coming and going.

It should have calmed her. It didn't. She kept seeing the words of that stupid note. *"In case of my demise"*—who ever used such a word?—*"tell her I tried to get back."* Dead or alive, he promised he'd get back.

Who wanted him back dead?

She flung over to her side, trying to get comfortable, and mentally counted her savings. Calculated how much she would need to earn in just over a week. It was hopeless, but nevertheless, she considered every possibility. It was not something that particularly soothed her thoughts, but it beat thinking about Levi.

Next morning the children could barely wait to get their

clothes on before they begged to be able to hurry down to watch the ferry. "He'll come today," Emmy insisted.

"We can't be sure. We'll have to wait and see." Glory wanted to prepare the child for disappointment.

Emmy simply tossed her head and ignored Glory's warning. "I'm tired of waiting."

If only life was so easy. Even trusting God appeared to come with challenges and disappointments. Last night she'd read a verse in Job, chapter thirteen, verse fifteen, *"Though he slay me, yet will I trust in him."* And seems God almost slew Job. Took his children, his cattle, everything. Still Job trusted God. Glory didn't know if she could do the same given the same circumstances.

The kids scampered ahead of her to a spot where they could watch people crossing on the ferry, mostly heading north. She sat with them to watch. And wait. So Emmy was tired of waiting, was she? Glory could tell her she might be in for a lifetime of waiting unless she put the past behind her.

And yet, Glory prayed inwardly Levi would return—alive. With Mr. Templeton at his side.

Midmorning she watched him ride to the landing site of the ferry on the far side of the river. He looked like he'd been battered mercilessly. It showed in the way his shoulders slumped, his hat tipped forward over his forehead hiding his eyes from onlookers. He rode alone and Glory knew it meant bad news of one sort or another.

The children had grown bored and played with rocks in the grass, pretending to herd them like a bunch of horses.

Glory didn't point out Levi to them. They'd have to face the bad news soon enough.

At the sound of the ferry beaching on this side of the river, they sat up and immediately saw Levi on Billy Bob. As quickly they saw that he was alone.

Jack sprang to his feet.

Emmy shrank into the grass, her hand pressed to her mouth.

Glory waited, not sure if she should urge them toward the ferry or wait for Levi to ride to them. But already Levi was headed their direction. She rose to wait by the children.

Levi swung from his horse and made the last few steps on foot. He stood before them, pushed his hat back to reveal a face wreathed in anguish and disappointment.

"You didn't find him, did you?" Jack's voice rang with resignation.

Levi squatted to Jack's level. "I'm sorry. I did find him. But he won't be coming back."

"He's dead, ain't he?" Jack bunched his fists at his side. He tried for anger, but his voice quivered.

"Yes." Levi pulled the boy into his arms and let Jack weep against his shoulder.

Glory sat beside Emmy and opened her arms.

Tears streaming down her face, Emmy climbed to Glory's lap and wrapped her arms about her neck. Hot tears soaked Glory's shoulder.

She didn't mind in the least and held Emmy close, her own eyes clouding with tears. It was even worse than knowing her pa was out there and didn't care to come back. Their pa would never come back. No false hopes. No eternal waiting.

She closed her eyes and rocked the child.

Now what?

eleven

Levi scrubbed his chin, noted the rasping. He needed a shave. But it was the least of things he needed. He'd hoped for a different outcome, but there was no way to change things.

It had been a tough day. The children were understandably upset and required attention from both him and Glory.

"I couldn't have made it through this day without you." His weariness made his voice hoarse.

They stood at the side of the bed watching the children who had finally fallen asleep. His shoulder almost touched Glory's. He wanted to find comfort in holding her, wanted to tell her the whole sorry story. "Let's go sit outside. We'll be able to hear them if they call out but won't disturb them as we talk."

She nodded, grabbed a chair, and carried it to the side of the shop.

He followed, also carrying a chair, and parked it close to hers, grateful when she made no protest or shifted farther away.

For a moment they sat in silence. The lowering sun sent pink coloring into the clouds. The tree-covered hills turned a deep green, almost black. He leaned back and tried to think of nothing but the beauty of the sky, the sureness of God's love. It was hard to concentrate on either after his trip.

"Was it awful?"

Glory's quiet question shuddered through him. "It wasn't fun. I don't know what I expected. Maybe he was injured and couldn't get back."

"I guess dead is about as injured as you can get."

He understood that she hoped to make him smile and he appreciated her efforts, but he wasn't ready to enjoy any humor.

She studied him, and he let her without meeting her look. "What happened?"

"The children told me he'd hurried away to return a package a fellow traveler had forgotten. That much I knew. What I didn't know, and neither did he, was the package had been stolen from a rough pair of men. When they saw Mr. Templeton with it, they took him as well as the package. According to what others had observed, they had crossed into the British territories. I followed, always asking about the three men I sought. I heard clues but never saw them." He closed his eyes and tipped his head back. "I kept thinking how desperate Mr. Templeton must be, knowing his kids were waiting for him back near Bonners Ferry. Knowing how small and vulnerable they were."

She touched his arm. "Too bad he couldn't have known they were safe with you."

He lowered his head to see her hand on his arm. It steadied him, made it possible for him to fill his lungs without the air catching halfway down. "I went to the Mounted Police to ask if they had any word on the man I sought. Unfortunately they did. They'd buried the man."

She pressed her hand more firmly to his arm, causing his blood to flow more smoothly through his veins. He knew he was imagining it, but that was how it felt.

"They had written a report. They gave me a copy." He touched the inner pocket of his vest where the pages waited to be passed on to someone who would someday tell the children the whole truth. "There was a fight. It seems Mr. Templeton saw his chance to escape his captors and stood up before a crowd of witnesses and said he was being held against his will. He had two children needing a father and waiting for him to return. They'd been waiting ten days and it was too long for youngsters to be alone. He had to get back to them and called upon those present to witness his escape and help him return. Of course the crowd surged forward, intent on punishing the two culprits, but they escaped, leaving Mr. Templeton behind. People provided him with a horse, supplies, and everything else he needed to get back here." It should have been the happy ending to the whole affair. "He was found two days later. Shot in the back. He was on his way here."

"Did they catch the men?"

"No, but the Mounted Police vow they will be captured and brought to justice."

"Good." She leaned back and pulled her hand away.

His arm felt cold and heavy. His heart empty just because he no longer had the comfort of her touch. He thought of the time he had taken a kiss. Wished he could take another.

"I'm sorry," she murmured. "Sorry for you. Sorry the man died. Sorry for the kids." Her voice choked off.

He turned to her and opened his arms, more than half-expecting she would laugh and jerk away, but she came readily, wrapping her arms around his waist and holding him. He pressed his cheek to her hair and breathed in the warm, earthy scent of her. He couldn't say if she held him or he held her, only it eased the pain that had become a knot in his chest.

He didn't want to let her go, didn't want to tell her what else he'd learned, but she shifted and tipped her head to look into his face. Did he see longing in her eyes? Or was he only dreaming it, wishing for it?

"Glory," he whispered and slowly lowered his head, giving her a moment to pull away if she didn't want him to kiss her. She didn't move, and he almost smiled before he caught her lips in a gentle kiss. This one was mutual, not stolen. Prickly Miss Glory was kissing him.

She broke away. Sat up. Patted her hair and faced forward.

He cupped her shoulder. "Thank you."

The look she gave him encompassed so many things. Surprise, denial, and a healthy dose of interest causing her to glance at his mouth and jerk away as soon as she did, as if denying she might have liked it just a little.

"Glory, I appreciate your kindness in offering me sympathy." It was best for them both if they believed it had been nothing more.

But she snorted. "Is that what it was?"

It's what it had to be though Levi wished otherwise. He hoped Matt would appreciate the sacrifices Levi was making on his behalf. He had chosen a hard road but would not forget the verse that said, *"No man, putting his hand to the plough, and looking back, is fit for the kingdom of God."* He would not look back or regret his vow. "I asked about your pa while I was up north."

She stiffened and her expression informed him she didn't care. Almost he believed her, but she could not hide the flash of pain in her eyes.

"The Mounted Police had heard of him. Said he was headed for the gold fields farther west. I asked them to forward a message if they heard anything more."

Glory pressed her palms together and clamped her hands between her knees. She sat forward not moving, not saying anything, not revealing a single emotion.

"Glory, at least you know he's still alive."

She flung him a gaze rife with anger and pain and so much more. "It would be easier if he was dead. No more waiting. No more wondering if we might get a message like the one you brought the children. It would be over." She bent over her knees and sat as still as a statue.

He could see only the back of her neck and the heavy brown braid hanging over her shoulder. He lifted the braid and moved it to the other side, hoping he could see her face but got only a glimpse of her profile as she shifted away. "Glory, it's always better to know."

She didn't reply or even move.

"Glory?"

Slowly she sat upright, and when she looked at him, her face was set in a hard line, silently informing him she didn't want to discuss it. She didn't thank him for asking after her pa and definitely did not agree it was better to know. "What are you going to do about the children now?"

He sucked in air, found the knot in his chest had returned. What had he expected? That she would throw herself in his arms in gratitude? Yes, he would like her to be a little grateful. God forgive him. He couldn't seem to remember his vow when he was with Glory. Nor was it possible to avoid thinking of her more deeply than he should.

He was still certain she was part of his mission in Bonners Ferry. But he no longer knew how. To reform her seemed unnecessary. She had simply adjusted to her life in the only way that made sense to her. And it now made sense to him as well. She rescued horses because she knew what it was like to be hurt and afraid. And despite the way his heart ached to rescue her, it wasn't possible. He would never regret his vow or change his mind about it.

He forced his thoughts to her question. "I asked Jack about family. He said they have grandparents back in San Francisco. I'm going to write them and inform them of the children's situation. If they are the caring sort, they will make arrangements."

"Let's hope they are."

"More than that, let's pray they are."

She studied him a moment. "There are times I forget about prayer." She continued to look into his eyes as if searching for a hidden truth. "I have trouble believing in prayer when things don't go the way I think they should."

"There's a verse in Psalm one hundred and thirty-nine that comforts me when I feel like I'm alone in the dark, that God has forsaken me. It says, 'The darkness and the light are both alike to thee.' He is still there even when we can't see it. Sometimes He is perhaps testing us to see if we love Him only for what He can give us or because of what He's already done for us."

"I read something in Job." She told him of the verse. "I don't like to think God would send trouble to my life just to see if I will continue to love Him."

"I don't have the answers. I wish I did. But I struggle with the same things. Are troubles meant to test us? Or are they simply a part of living on this earth and God gives us what we need to get through them?"

"Maybe it's both."

"Maybe." He recognized something still troubled her.

"What if. . ." Her voice fell to a whisper. "What if God is like Pa and can't be counted on?"

He reached for her hands and held them between his. "God is not a man that He changes His mind or has regrets. He says He loves us with an everlasting love. He is the same yesterday, today, and forever. His love is the one constant that never changes."

A slow smile drove away the tension in her face. "Everlasting. Always the same. I can trust Him whatever happens."

"You can indeed." He released her hands and let the words sift through his own thoughts. Whatever God had in store for him, however hard it was, he did not face it alone. God would guide him through this long ache of wishing he could love Glory. Knowing he could not and still keep his vow. And he intended to keep his vow.

My service for Matt's salvation. That's what he'd said and renounced all else, including love and marriage.

❧

Glory had sold two of the horses and put the money in her coffee can, but the two weeks was up and she did not have enough to purchase the land. *Master* Milton had left town days ago. *God, help the man to stay away until I can earn enough money.*

She had neglected the horses while caring for the children, and much of the work she'd accomplished with Big Gray had come undone. But she had plenty of patience to continue winning the animal's trust. She'd considered other pieces of land and dismissed them for various reasons—not enough pasture, too far from town for her to go back and forth each day, down in the flats where it was damp underfoot. She wouldn't put her horses there and risk damaging their hooves.

As she worked, she mentally recounted the events of the previous days. The children alternately played happily and then retreated into sadness. Levi was good with them. Holding them as they cried. Not telling them it would be all right. Losing both parents would never be all right, and if the grandparents didn't come, life could get much harder.

These kids were innocent and didn't deserve this misfortune. Sometimes it was hard to trust God. But she could hardly blame God that wicked men chose to do evil. Or even that ordinary men did ordinary things that hurt others. Like Pa chasing after fortune and leaving three little girls to fend for themselves. Despite the neglect, the three little girls had grown into three self-sufficient women. So she had that to be grateful for.

She finished working with the horses and went to her favorite spot to sit and look over the valley. The sound of an approaching horse drew her attention to the trail. It was a big, black horse carrying a man wearing a buckskin vest. What was Levi doing here? He'd never visited this place before. She watched him unobserved for a few minutes. She no longer doubted he was a real preacher, even if he did wear a fringed vest. It was just something he liked wearing even as she liked wearing britches. Britches were convenient, too, when working with the horses.

She allowed herself to admire the way he sat Billy Bob. The way his eyes roamed his surroundings, how the blue of the sky reflected in his eyes as he turned toward the light. He had a good face. One that would grow old in a good way. For the first time in her life, Glory thought about growing old with such a man at her side.

She jerked her thoughts back to being sensible. He'd made it as clear as the air around her he had no such interest in her. Even apologized for saying he cared. A man couldn't get much more direct than that. It didn't matter to her. She would not be trusting a man to love her always.

But if she did, it would be a man like Levi.

Her throat closed off, and her eyes grew damp. Even though she vigorously denied it, she could imagine sharing her life with Levi. Actually ached to do so. It took half a dozen deep breaths to cleanse herself of such nonsense.

And just in time.

Levi saw her in the shade of the tree and slid off his horse without using the stirrups in a way that seemed impossibly smooth. "Didn't expect to see you here."

"I could say the same about you."

"Thought I'd ride up and have a look around. May I join you?" He indicated the ground beside her.

"Ground is free," she said, "just like the sky and air. Help yourself."

He chuckled. "It would kill you to say, 'Please, sit down, and welcome,' wouldn't it?"

"Not quite." She grinned at him. They seemed to have arrived at a new place in their friendship—acknowledging it existed, setting boundaries to protect them both. Boundaries of humor and common interests.

He sank down beside her, his shoulder pressed to hers as they shared the support of the tree. She allowed herself to enjoy the strength of him at her side.

Neither of them spoke, and Glory enjoyed a sense of contentment. He was a good man. Caring. Willing to go the extra mile for others. The sort of man a person could learn to lean on. And she let her body settle toward him. "What did you do with Emmy and Jack?"

"Left them with Toby. He was building a fort in the trees behind the stopping house when I left."

"Sounds like fun."

"All three were excited about the prospect."

It was pleasant and warm. She was glad there seemed nothing to disagree about at the moment. "No word from the grandparents?"

"Not yet."

"What if—"

He squeezed her hand. "Let's not build bridges across rivers before we need them."

Her heart curled around his fingers and settled down for a long stay. Her head told her it was only a friendly gesture, but inside her heart something more was going on. She had to know why he couldn't care about her because frankly she didn't believe it. He cared even as he denied it. "Why did you decide to become a preacher?"

"I told you. My grandfather was a preacher. I sort of inherited the job, I suppose."

She shifted so she could see his face, study his eyes. "I don't see you deciding to do something simply because your grandfather did. There's something more, isn't there?" The way his eyes flicked toward her and then jerked away, she knew she had guessed correctly. "I'm right. I know I am. So what's the big secret?"

He slowly brought his blue gaze toward her and searched long and hard. She allowed him to explore deeper into who she was than anyone had ever before. He held her in his steady look and slowly nodded. "I made a vow."

A vow? "What sort of vow?"

"I want my brother to come back."

"I don't understand."

"I can't explain." He jumped to his feet. "Come on. Let's look around." He pulled her to his side.

So he didn't want to tell her. No reason it should matter. But it did. She didn't care for secrets. They made a person uneasy. Distrustful even. Not that she was prepared to trust him.

Except she was. At some point, and she couldn't say when or where it had happened, she'd decided the man was too kind to be the Rawhide Kid. She'd let herself trust.

A shiver of fear trickled up her spine. Trusting opened the door to disappointment. "You plan to be around here long?"

"Thinking of staying a long time. I'd like to start a mission. You know, a home for unfortunates like Widow Kish, children like Emmy and Jack, and even sick people needing care like Mr. Phelps. Right now there is no place for them. If I had a little piece of land, I'd build such a house and a church."

Would he want a wife to share the work? She glanced down at her britches. Like Joanna said, Glory wasn't the sort of woman a preacher man would choose. Perhaps it explained why he couldn't let himself care. Maybe if she wore a dress. . .

"I heard there was a piece of land up here for sale."

She ground to a halt and tore her hand from his. "Who said?"

"There's a notice in the store. Owner is a Mr. Milton. It's this land right here. It's a perfect place for a mission. Close enough to town to go back and forth, high enough to be dry, and a beautiful view. Look, there's a FOR SALE sign on it."

She pushed by him and stared at the sign nailed to the tree of her pasture. When had it been plastered there and why hadn't she noticed it?

Because the man had been careful to nail it just out of sight of a person going to the pasture where she kept her horses. She ripped the sign from the tree and threw it on the ground. "This is my land. Look." She pointed. "Those are my horses." The animals grazed contentedly a few yards from the trail.

"I don't understand. Why would someone try and sell land you own?"

"Because," she spat out the words, "I haven't come up with enough money to pay for it."

"So it is for sale?"

She faced him, letting every disappointment, every failure of every man she'd ever experienced burn across his cheeks. "If you buy my land I will never forgive you. Never."

He reached for her, but she sidestepped, avoiding his touch. "Glory, I'll find another piece of land."

"You won't find one as nice as this."

"Probably not, but I have no desire to hurt you. Only thing is. . ."

She waited for his excuses.

"What's to stop someone else from buying it?"

"I'm praying for God to help me. Surely He'll answer." She

hated how desperate she sounded.

"Glory, I—" He lifted his hands in defeat. "God doesn't promise to always give us what we want. He promises to give us what we need. And to always love us."

Her heart faltered as she thought of Job's words. "This is what I need. I'm sure God knows it."

"I guess the question is, will you still trust Him even if you don't get the land?"

Her eyes grew brittle. "Will you still trust Him if your brother doesn't come back?"

She wanted to feel victory at the uncertainty in his face, but all she felt was a long ache. "Trusting isn't so easy, is it?"

"I never said it was. But the option of trusting no one and nothing isn't appealing. Far better to trust a God of love."

All her fight evaporated. "I will continue to pray."

"I will pray for the same thing."

"What about your mission?"

He smiled. "There must be something almost as nice as this. Will you help me look?"

"Of course." Her world felt brighter. Her land was safe for now, and Levi wasn't angry with her.

"Then let's go."

"Right now?"

"You got something better to do with your time?"

She could think of nothing at all she'd sooner do, so she whistled for Pal, and side-by-side she and Levi rode higher looking at other sites. They crossed back and forth. She'd looked at all this and knew her way around. But it had not been nearly as much fun when she'd ridden around these places on her own. Now discussing the land, the view, the possibilities with Levi made it much more interesting.

By the time the afternoon headed toward supper, they had examined much land.

"There's a few places that could work. But you're right, nothing is as nice as your pasture."

"I told you so," she crowed.

"I'm sure we'll find something. Will you help me again tomorrow?"

They had reached the shop and headed the horses into the little bit of pasture. He dropped to the ground in the same fluid motion she'd admired so many times and reached up to lift her down. She wanted to protest. Hadn't needed anyone lifting her down for many years. But he didn't give her a chance.

He lowered her to the ground and stood facing her. "Thank you for your help, and I hope you get your dreams. I really do." He bent closer.

She knew he was going to kiss her and she welcomed it. But he only brushed his lips to her forehead. Annoyed she demanded, "What was that?"

"Just a thank-you."

"Huh." She gave him a good view of her back as she turned to remove Pal's saddle. Just a thank-you? She deserved a whole lot more than that. And wanted it.

She hustled her gear into the shop, resisting the urge to kick herself at each step. What she wanted was contrary to all the promises she'd made to herself. And he'd made it clear he wasn't interested in the likes of her. She was not suitable as a preacher's wife. She understood it. Too bad he didn't think to ask if she could change, because she just might be willing to give it a try.

If he needed her to be a lady, she could do it.

twelve

They spent three days riding about the country looking at land. Glory realized at some point finding a suitable location for his mission had taken second place to spending time together, although Levi didn't say anything or give her reason to think he was reconsidering his earlier declaration he couldn't care about her. He didn't try and kiss her again. . .and she told herself she wasn't disappointed because the way he looked at her made her feel ten feet tall. She often brought along a light lunch and they shared it, usually with their backs pressed to a tree, their shoulders brushing.

Today he suggested they go to the pasture where she kept her horses. "I like the view from there."

So they rode up the hill and returned to her favorite spot. They sat and enjoyed the scenery for about thirty seconds then Levi pulled a letter from his inside vest pocket. "I heard from the grandparents."

Did he sound pleased or disappointed? She couldn't tell, but then it could be that her own fears for the future of the children made her blind and deaf. "I'm afraid to ask what they said." So many times she'd seen a letter arrive and Joanna tear it open. Each time she'd crossed her fingers behind her back and hoped it was from Pa, saying he would be there within the week. Seldom did they receive such welcome news. Almost always he was simply informing them he was going somewhere else, leaving them to either stay where they were or find a way to follow him. They usually did the latter, never quite catching up to him but being on his heels.

"It's good news. They're coming to personally get the children. That way we'll be able to meet them and judge for ourselves if they'll make a good home for the children."

"And if you think otherwise?"

"It's not like we could do anything about it, but I hope and pray they are kind. It would make it easier to let them go if we could think they were."

She thought of his statement. *"It's not like we could do anything about it. . ."* She knew it revealed a lot about Levi. From the little he'd said, she knew life with his strict grandparents had been difficult. But it was a home, and he'd made the best of it. It made her feel a strange twist of both admiration and sympathy. "When are they arriving?"

"They'll be here tomorrow."

"Do they say how long they'll stay?"

"No. It's going to be hard to say good-bye to the kids." He faced her. "But at least they have family. What about those who don't? I have such a burden for orphaned children. And for people like Widow Kish with no home. Not every widow ends up remarried and taken care of. I want to help people who need it, but I need a place for them to live."

Seeing the way his concern drove worry lines across his forehead, she squeezed his forearm, liking the warmth of his skin through the fabric of his shirt.

He glanced about. "I need to find suitable land and build a house."

"We'll find something suitable. I know it." She pressed harder against the tree as she thought of how the land she hoped to buy was so ideal.

He chuckled and reached for her hand. "I'm not going to steal your land. I promise."

She let him take her hand. Pushed aside her fears and doubts. After all, hadn't she decided to trust God? And somehow that enabled her to trust Levi.

"I haven't told the children yet. I suppose I should." He pushed to his feet. "Do you want to come with me?"

"Yes. . .but I can't. I have to feed the horses and see they have water." And spend some time working with them. She'd neglected them the last few days.

"Of course. Come and see me when you get back to town, and I'll tell you how it went." He stuffed the letter back inside his vest and strode away.

She remained where she was, soaking up the view and remembering all the other views she and Levi had enjoyed. A sense of peace and rightness filled her. But she couldn't sit there all day dreaming. The animals did need attention. She pushed to her feet, dusted her backside, and headed for the pasture.

Something on the ground next to where Levi had tied Billy Bob caught her attention. A piece of paper. He must have dropped the letter when he tried to put it in his pocket.

She scooped up the paper. It was the wrong shape and size to be the letter. Curious, she unfolded it. It took her several seconds to believe she held a wanted poster. Even then she couldn't believe the identity of the man on the poster.

Her heart stopped beating. Her lungs stopped working. Seems her ears must have stopped working, too, because a vast silence surrounded her, and then everything started up with a bang. She gasped as her heart kicked against her ribs and her ears roared.

"It can't be," she whispered. But there was no mistaking the likeness, even though it was only a drawing. It was Levi. The Rawhide Kid. Reward of $500. Toby had been right in his first observation.

She stared at the poster a long time, her thoughts scrambling in a thousand different directions.

He was living a lie.

But he was a good man.

The reward money would buy her land.

Who would do the good things he did if she turned him in for the money? Who would be her friend?

What was she going to do?

Finally, she folded the poster and carefully slid it into her pocket. Levi had obviously changed his mind and left his life of crime. Didn't everyone deserve a chance to start over? If he could do it, so could she.

After taking care of the horses, she returned to town, went immediately to the store, and placed a mail order for a dress. The storekeeper promised he wouldn't tell anyone.

Only then did she go to find Levi.

❧

Levi waited for the grandparents in front of the store. They would arrive by private buggy, hired out of Sandpoint. Being reunited with the grandparents was best for the kids. Yet he hoped the grandparents weren't like the ones he'd had to live with.

He often wondered how his fun-loving, happy ma could have been the product of that home. It had been all about rules governing every minute of the day. As if making any sort of decision was a sin.

Small wonder Matt had rebelled. Trouble was, Matt's rebellion had gone too far. He could have left home and sought his own path without crossing into lawlessness. Levi sighed. Anger had driven Matt to make foolish choices.

A buggy approached, and Levi snatched his hat from his head. He squinted, trying to see the couple, gauge what sort they were. But dust billowed up as the buggy slowed, obscuring any sight of the occupants. He stepped back and waited for the dust to settle and glanced back to the figure watching out the window.

He'd asked Glory to join him, but she'd laughed and refused. She'd said, "I might ruin your good impression on them," then glanced down at her britches. "After all, they'll be measuring you up as surely as you're measuring them." So instead of being by his side she watched from the protection of the store. He'd wanted to say she would pass inspection just as she was, but she hadn't given him the chance.

He smiled at her now, hoping she would read in his look his acceptance. He didn't know when he'd decided he didn't have any intention of trying to reform her. She was fine just the way she was. . .britches and all.

By the time he turned back to the buggy, a stately looking gentleman assisted a black-clad woman from the back. He strode forward and introduced himself.

It was much later, after supper taken at the stopping house, before he got a chance to speak to Glory alone.

"They seem nice enough, don't you agree?" They had left the grandparents to put the children to bed and spend the night with them. Levi would sleep under the stars. Not something he minded at all.

They had walked to a place overlooking the river and found a spot to sit and watch the sun set.

Glory didn't answer for a moment, as if considering her words. "I guess we have to trust what they are when they're here is what they are when they aren't here."

He chuckled. "And you don't know if you can trust them or not."

"Trust is a pretty fragile thing. I don't give it easily."

"But when you do?" Did he hope to hear her say she trusted him? Yes, he wanted it, but for all the wrong reasons. Maybe not wrong, but not available for him. He would not forget Matt in prison, not even for the joy of knowing a woman like Glory—spunky, free-thinking, and independent.

A rescuer of abused animals. . .and so much more he couldn't let himself enumerate because of the way it made him struggle to remember his vow.

"All I can say is there are no second chances."

She must mean her father. "That's pretty harsh. What if your pa comes back a reformed man? Wouldn't you give him another chance?"

"I no longer even think about Pa that way. He's just a person we're related to. Nothing more. As such, if he came back half-dead, I'd care for him. Just as I would any sick or injured person or animal."

"But without forgiving him?"

She didn't answer, and he supposed that was her answer. Then she spoke, quietly, softly. "I will never say never."

It was a huge concession on her part. One that made him realize just how much she'd grown in her faith. He reached for her hand. "Perhaps you will get the chance to take never out of your life one of these days."

She gave him a long, considering look. "Maybe I already have."

"Really? How? When?"

She shrugged. "Can't say. Just have."

He wanted to hug her, dance her across the prairie, but he didn't have the right, so he squeezed her shoulders with one arm. "You've changed, Glory Hamilton."

"You have no idea how much."

He ached clear through that he didn't have the right to ask if her change included trusting him. Instead, he shifted the conversation back to the children. "The children are a little tense around the grandparents, but that would seem normal considering they haven't seen them in several years and it signals the reality of their father's death."

"How long are the grandparents staying?" she asked.

"Mrs. Templeton said she needed a few days to recuperate before she makes the return trip. They said they'd like me to show them around, explain the work I want to do."

"They'll be here Sunday then?"

"At least that long."

"So they'll hear you preach?"

He wondered why the caution in her voice. "Don't you think that's a good thing?" Did she consider him a poor preacher? It wasn't something they'd ever discussed, and suddenly he longed to know. "You think they'll be disappointed when they hear me?"

"No, I didn't mean that. I think you're a very good preacher. I remember the first Sunday." She gave a low laugh. "I thought you'd preach fire and brimstone and warn people like me we needed to toe the line."

His laugh was mocking. "I wanted to. But I couldn't. Now I know you only want to shock people to keep them at a distance and protect yourself."

She grew very still. "Is that what I do?"

Had he gone too far? Crossed her solid fence lines?

A deep sigh shuddered from her. "I suppose I do. I just never thought of it. Maybe I can change."

"How?"

"You know. Be more ladylike. That sort of thing." She sounded as if the words burned her tongue.

"Glory, who you are is who you are and is just fine. All you can do is learn to trust others. Or at least God."

"You think that's all I need?"

"I know it."

She sighed, a sound as full of uncertainty as any he'd heard.

❧

By the time Sunday rolled around, Levi had taken the Templetons around the country. They'd discussed the mission he wanted to start. They'd enjoyed several picnics with the children. Levi was convinced they would be good with the children, who were anxious to get to their new home.

Mr. Templeton had promised they'd leave the next day if all went well. "I have some business to attend to before we leave."

Levi couldn't help wonder what business he could possibly have, but it wasn't his place to ask and he didn't.

Attendance had grown steadily at the Sunday service. From his place before the gathering audience, he looked about, saw the usual townspeople, as well as a number of people passing through, many whom had spent the night at the stopping house. Glory and her sisters had not yet appeared.

He picked up his Bible and quickly reviewed his notes.

A sudden rumble of murmurs made him glance up. He saw people looked to the right and followed the direction.

Three women approached. He recognized Mandy and Joanna, but the third was unfamiliar. No. Wait. It was Glory. In a dress. A very pretty dress. She had fashioned her braid around her head in a coronet.

Levi stared.

Glory sent him a defensive, vulnerable look then stared straight ahead.

Glory in a dress. He tried to think if he liked it. He didn't. Glory belonged in britches. Was there something wrong with him to think so? Shouldn't he be glad to see her in something more conventional? But he wasn't. This was not the Glory he knew and loved. Why would she change?

The question badgered the back of his thoughts as she and her sisters found a place to sit, as he led the singing, and even as he delivered his sermon.

He wanted to ask her, but several people spoke to him after the service, and he had to watch Glory and her sisters slip away. As soon as he could get away, he hurried to the stopping house and burst into the kitchen. "Where's Glory?"

Joanna looked up from doing some mending. "She left. Try her shop."

He raced to the shop. Pal was gone, but he checked inside anyway just to make sure Glory wasn't there. She wasn't. He wanted to ride out and find her, but he'd promised the children to spend the afternoon with them.

And then Mrs. Templeton prepared a nice supper. "If all goes well this will be our last day here. I hope we can start our return journey tomorrow."

Levi could not excuse himself without seeming rude. But as soon as he could get away, he ran back to the stopping house, again demanding to see Glory.

Joanna shrugged. "She's not here."

"Is she avoiding me?"

"I'm not sure. Maybe she's avoiding everyone."

"Why?"

"Why is she avoiding people or why did she wear a dress?"

"Yes."

Joanna chuckled. "The first is because of the last. But why she felt the need to don a dress? Well, I expect it has something to do with you."

"Me?" He backed up two steps as if she'd punched him in the chest.

"You being a preacher and all, I'm guessing she thought she had to be a proper lady before you'd look at her in that. . . you know. . .special way. And if you hurt my sister, you'll be answering to me."

Levi stumbled from the house. He'd told her he wasn't free to care. How had his vow turned into such a sacrifice? Was this God testing him?

He'd find her tomorrow and explain his vow. Tell her the

whole truth. She'd understand.

Only the next day turned into a blur of activities he couldn't escape.

Mr. Templeton disappeared right after breakfast, and when Levi tried to slip away, Mrs. Templeton begged him to wait. "He'll be back soon, then we must be on our way. He'll want to see you before he leaves."

Levi expected the man wanted to say a last good-bye, but it was all Levi could do to endure the wait.

Mr. Templeton strode in a short while later, a glow of victory on his face. "I did it, Mother. Just as we planned."

The pair grinned at each other then faced Levi. Mr. Templeton spoke, but it was obviously for the both of them. "We appreciate how you rescued our grandchildren, and we think you are doing a good work here. So to show our gratitude and help your cause, we bought land you can use to start your mission."

Levi knew his mouth hung open. He cranked it closed. Forced himself to speak. "You bought land?"

"We studied the options as you showed us around and did some asking around. There's one piece of land that seemed superior to all the others. It's close to town, high enough to not suffer floods, and it's beautiful. We purchased it and have put your name on the deed."

Levi's heart thudded to the soles of his boots and lay there quivering. "What land did you buy?"

"A piece owned by a Mr. Milton." They handed him a piece of paper he knew was the deed.

The deed to land he had promised Glory he would not buy. She would never understand.

He must find her and explain before she heard the news from another source. But he could not rush away until he'd helped the Templetons pack up everything, until he'd seen them safely into the hired buggy, until he'd said his final good-bye. His heart felt pulled in two as he kissed the children good-bye. "I'm going to miss you both."

Emmy hugged him tight. "I wish you could go with us."

He nodded and hugged Jack who tried to be brave about this parting, but tears glistened in his eyes as he broke away from Levi's arms. Levi's own eyes weren't without unshed tears. "Keep in touch," he said to the grandparents, and they promised they would.

He waved to them through blurry vision until the dust obscured them from sight. Then he drew in a deep, steadying breath and turned his heart toward the other half of his pain. He must find Glory.

છે

He'd bought the land. Everyone in town knew it. And everyone seemed to think it was a good idea. Not one person, apart from her sisters, expressed concern about what she'd do with her livestock. They all agreed the work Levi intended to do was so noble it deserved every bit of sacrifice necessary.

She was the only one making any sacrifice. And not willingly. What would they all think if she posted the wanted poster by the door of the general store? They wouldn't likely be so oh-isn't-Levi-wonderful then.

The paper practically burned a hole in her britches. She'd kept his secret because she thought he deserved a second chance. Now she knew he was more false than any of them knew.

There was something better than tacking the poster to the wall. She dug out an envelope and paper from the drawer where Joanna kept such things. She wrote a short note, addressed the envelope to the territorial marshal, and put in the wanted poster. Her footsteps driven by anger and a sense of betrayal, she delivered the letter to the ferry man.

She then rode out to her horses and led them from the pasture. For two cents she'd ride five days and disappear into the mountains far to the north.

Just like her pa.

She swallowed a bitter taste. If she left, it would be to run from deceit and lies. Why did Pa run when he had three daughters who had once longed for him to be part of their lives?

No more. No more trusting anything a man said or promised. She should have learned that lesson well enough from her father. Only it appeared she hadn't, and now she had to learn it over again. . .thanks to Levi.

Levi. She tried to think his name with the same coolness she thought of Pa, but instead it caught like a burr in her brain and scratched along her thoughts, leaving a trail of scraped flesh. She narrowed her eyes, ground down on her teeth, and tried to ignore it, but she suspected it would take a long time for the bruises to heal.

She left the gate of her pasture open and headed away from town without a backward look, her horses trailing after her. Properties she'd dismissed as being too far from town now seemed not nearly far enough, and she rode for two hours before she turned off the narrowing trail and ducked through crowded trees with barely enough room for a horse.

Fifteen yards later she broke into a grassy clearing. It didn't receive as much sunshine as her former pasture and would likely be dampish, but it was the best she could do. She strung rope from tree to tree, creating a temporary enclosure for the horses, then pulled her camping supplies from Pal's back. She hadn't come right out and told Joanna she wouldn't be back but had given enough hints that when she didn't return Joanna would understand.

Not until she sorted out her feelings, her sense of having

been dealt a dirty deal, would she return to town. Treacherous Levi intended to stay in town, but soon the marshal would ride in and take him away. Only then would Glory go back.

She sat staring at the horses munching down grass with little concern for their future. Her heart felt like a giant fist grinding against everything she valued, trusted, or even dreamed of.

Was she as much a traitor as Levi to turn him in?

But he was a criminal with a price on his head. And she needed the money to buy land. Perhaps she could even buy back *her* land.

If he had known she found the wanted poster, would he have trusted her to keep his secret?

Just like she'd trusted him. And look how that turned out.

She would never trust again.

What about God? Did her decision include God?

The words she'd read so many times in Job, and wondered at how the man could still trust God, crowded her mind. *"Though he slay me, yet will I trust in him."* Job was a better person than she. She couldn't find it in her heart to say, "Okay, it's fine," when everything was wrong.

❧

She spent her days working with the horses and sitting next to her campfire, which for the most part remained dead, and staring into space. She was healing, she told herself. Rebuilding the protective barriers around her heart she'd foolishly let crumble under Levi's influence.

Three days later she still had not returned to town. She'd worked with the horses all morning and at high noon sat by the cold fire chewing on dried biscuits when the sound of a footfall only inches away brought her to her feet, her hands out ready to defend herself.

Mandy broke into the clearing, laughing at Glory's alarm.

"I almost snuck up on you."

Glory blew out air as her lungs started to work again. "One of these days you're going to get yourself shot."

"You think I'd sneak up on someone I didn't know?"

"What are you doing here? How did you find me?"

Mandy snorted. "I could have tracked you across rocks. If you really wanted to disappear you wouldn't have dragged a herd of horses after you."

"I wasn't trying to disappear." At least not permanently.

Mandy looked around the clearing. "Not a bad place you got here. Maybe I'll join you." Then as almost an afterthought, "There's someone looking for you in town."

"Levi? I don't care to see him."

"It's a marshal. He says he needs to see you."

Glory jerked back. "Did he—?" Arrest Levi. But she couldn't say the words aloud. "Did he say what he wanted?"

Mandy widened her stance, crossed her arms over her chest, and studied Glory with narrowed eyes. "What have you done? Shot someone for whipping their horse? You haven't stolen a horse, have you?" She studied the placidly grazing horses as if trying to recall where Glory had gotten each. "Joanna sent me to find you and said if you did something that's going to get you arrested to shoot you on the spot. Do I need to get my gun?"

Glory laughed. She knew Joanna didn't mean it. It was her way of saying how angry she would be if Glory did something so stupid. "I didn't break any laws." She glanced around. "I guess the horses will be okay for a few hours." But there was only a rope keeping them from wandering away. "I'll have to come back as soon as I speak to the marshal."

In no hurry to return, welcoming any excuse for delay until it was almost three hours later, they rode into town.

A tall man, gun strapped to his hip, a star on his chest,

rose from a chair tipped back in front of her shop as they approached. He strode to the street and waited for them. "You must be Miss Glory Hamilton."

"Yup."

"You and I need to talk." He glanced about, suggesting they needed to talk in private.

"I'll let Joanna know I found you." Mandy rode toward the stopping house.

Glory slid from Pal's back and led the way to her shop. "We can talk here."

The marshal pulled the poster from his pocket, unfolded it, and spread it on her worktable. "This is the Rawhide Kid."

"I can read. I can also see the picture."

"The man in this picture is Matthew Powers."

It took a moment for the news to sink in. He lied about his name, too?

"Levi Powers's brother."

"Matt?"

"That's right. Though I can see why you might mistake the two. Heard they look a lot alike. Had to come and see for myself if it was true." The marshal folded the poster and handed it to Glory. "The Rawhide Kid is in prison as we speak."

She took the slip of paper with fingers almost lost at the end of arms that were long and heavy.

"I'll be leaving now." He paused. "Sure beats me how you couldn't see Levi Powers is a man you can trust." His departing footsteps echoed inside her hollowed-out thoughts.

Why couldn't she trust Levi?

She hadn't even given him a chance to explain about the wanted poster. Even as she hadn't given him a chance to explain about the land.

Sounds from the other side of the door to the room he

rented indicated he was there.

Swallowing her wrongful pride and hurt feelings, she acknowledged her lack of trust stemmed from years of learning she couldn't count on her father. Levi was not her father. And she was no longer a child.

She went outside and around to the outer door of the room. She knocked, and he called for her to enter.

She stepped inside and saw his saddlebags packed. A quick glance revealed he'd removed everything belonging to him. The room already had a deserted air. "Are you going somewhere?"

His face could have been a wooden mask for all he revealed. "I can't believe you thought I was the Rawhide Kid and sent for the marshal."

"It looks like you."

"Is that what you think of me? Is this because of the land?"

"You promised you wouldn't buy it."

"And I kept my promise."

"Funny then that there is a deed somewhere with your name on it."

"Mr. Templeton bought it as their way of saying thanks. I had no idea they planned to do so, and of course they had no way of knowing of my promise to you. Glory, I'm sorry it turned out this way." He took a step toward her, his expression regretful and so much more.

For a moment she let herself believe she saw caring and love in his face. Then he drew back and grabbed up the saddlebags and tossed them over his shoulder.

"Where are you going?" Was this how it would end? And it was all her fault. "I'm sorry. I realize I have to separate my experience with trusting Pa and being disappointed from other people." She swallowed hard knowing she had to say more. "From you."

"Glory, I have to go. There is something I need to do."

She couldn't beg. It made her too vulnerable.

He paused at her side. Again she let herself believe she saw tenderness and longing. Then he put that wooden mask in place again. "I'm going to see my brother. Feel free to take your horses back to the pasture. I won't be using it anytime soon."

Her feet might as well have been riveted to the floor. She couldn't make them move even when she heard him saddle his horse. Not even when she heard him mount, the leather creaking beneath his weight.

"Good-bye, Glory."

The words scraped her insides hollow.

The thud of Billy Bob's feet thundered through her, and she cried a protest. "Wait." She dashed for the door and around to the pen just in time to see him ride down the street, away from town.

He had not said if he would return.

She lurched against the splintery wall of the shop and leaned over as pain grabbed her insides. He was gone, and it was her fault for not trusting him.

thirteen

The realization she'd allowed her feelings about Pa cloud her reason had come too late. She should have trusted Levi. It was time to grow up. Even if it was too late with Levi, she had to stop looking at everything through the disappointment of Pa's continual disappearances. She had to trust God. Just like Job. Even when things weren't going the way she wanted.

Day after day Glory hurried through her chores. She did her work as always but far faster than before. All she wanted was to spend time with her horses and her thoughts. Joanna allowed her to take the Bible with her, and she spent hours reading it, finding solace in the words, the promises, God's love.

One side of her heart was empty and barren, filled with wind-driven regrets. The other side grew strong and sure of God's faithfulness.

The pasture was a temporary fix, but so far she had not come up with a permanent one. But she prayed about it and tried to trust God. Trusting still did not come easy. Perhaps it never would. She would always have to choose trust over doubt.

One question continued to weigh on her mind. Did she have the right to ask God to bring Levi back? Perhaps *right* was not the word she meant. Seems she didn't deserve anything from God, but He gave out of love. Maybe the question was, did she have the faith to ask God? More importantly, did she have the faith to trust God even if Levi didn't come? If her prayer wasn't answered the way she wanted?

It was a choice. And she chose to trust God no matter what the answer.

God, I messed up with Levi. I didn't trust him, and I should have. I'd like a chance to try again so I'm asking You to give me that chance. Send Levi back. Remind him of the work he has to do here. But whatever happens, I will trust You.

She sat as blessed peace filled the half of her heart that didn't miss Levi. Trust might be hard, but it sure felt better than anger. Feeling more settled than she had in a very long time, she returned to town to help Joanna.

As the days passed, she promised herself she wouldn't check down the road hoping to see Levi riding toward town, wouldn't check the horses hitched at the side of the street for Billy Bob, but she couldn't help herself. Each time she did and didn't see what she wanted to see, she reminded herself she would trust God no matter what.

Her inner peace grew, spilling into the empty half of her heart. But she knew it would never be completely satisfied without Levi to share her life.

&

Levi had returned from his trip. He'd been gone only ten days, but it seemed a lifetime, and he could hardly wait to see Glory. He hoped to find her up the hill with her horses and went there first. She sat on the edge of the property where they had shared so many good times, and he stood hidden in the shadows of some trees so he could watch her unobserved, gauge how she was. Whether or not she would give him a chance to explain himself or chase him off with a big stick.

She turned her face toward the sky. Her expression made his pulse feel as if he had been riding a smooth trail and suddenly his mount stepped into a dip, leaving his heart to follow in a desperate dive.

He had never seen her more beautiful, as if she captured

the sunshine inside her but couldn't keep it there. It breathed through her pores. He couldn't stop staring, couldn't move toward her. In fact, he couldn't think.

She grew watchful, seemed to listen to some silent voice within her.

He knew the moment she grew aware of his presence. She splayed her fingers to her chest as if she wondered if it was her imagination and she wanted to capture it and make it real. At least that was what he hoped the gesture meant. Then she jerked to the right and stared into the shadows.

He edged forward, hesitantly, not wanting to shatter the moment. It felt sacred, as if he'd entered a place of worship. *God, help me speak clearly and plainly. Help her understand.*

"Levi?" His name was a gentle whisper fluttering through the air and landing in his heart with force enough to make him think it should have been shouted. "I've been waiting for you," she murmured.

He didn't know what to make of that and couldn't ask. "Can we talk?"

She grinned. "Far as I know we're both very capable of it." She shifted and indicated the grass beside her.

"I want to explain."

"Sit down before I get a crick in my neck."

He sat though he wasn't sure she'd be so welcoming once he told his whole story.

"Go ahead and explain." She sounded half-teasing, half-exasperated.

"You had a right to wonder about me. I didn't tell you everything."

She sat quietly, giving him plenty of time to sort his thoughts.

Not that he needed time. He'd practiced his speech over and over since he left Matt at the territorial prison. Suddenly words seemed so inadequate. But words were all he had at this point.

"I should have told you the whole truth about Matt. How he didn't just rebel against our grandparents' rules. He rebelled against everything and became the Rawhide Kid, a wanted man. I suppose I didn't want to admit who he was. I didn't want people to think I was like my brother."

She drew in a breath as if she meant to speak.

"Let me finish before you say anything."

She nodded and let him go on.

"I should have told you the rest of it, too. You see, when I watched them drag Matt away in chains to serve his sentence, I made a vow to God. I said I would devote my life solely to serving God if He would work on Matt in prison. It was a foolish vow, one I probably shouldn't have made, but I did and I couldn't back out without perhaps angering God."

He held up a hand to silence her as she again started to speak. "It was foolish because I started to care about you and knew I didn't have the right. I had no idea how to change my vow. You don't vow something to God and then say, 'Oops, I changed my mind.'" He sorted out his thoughts, wondered how he could think this would be simple.

"When you thought I was the Rawhide Kid, I was shocked. I don't blame you. Matt and I do look alike. I understand your anger and how hard it is to trust. But how was I to tell you to trust me when I had no right to offer you anything? I had to find an answer or leave for good." He had struggled so hard, knowing he had made a vow with no reservations but aching to be free to love Glory. "I went to see Matt. I told him of my vow, told him that I had fallen in love and didn't know how to get out of the vow."

Her quick intake of breath brought a fleeting smile to his lips. Then he gave a sharp laugh. "Seems odd to seek counsel from someone in prison, but that's what I did."

"And?" She sounded as if she couldn't wait to hear if he found a solution.

"Matt had a good laugh at my expense. He wanted to know why I thought God owed me anything, and when I tried to deny it, he said that's what my vow was. He said I thought if I served God in the way I chose, sacrificing my chance to love and have a family, then God owed it to me to make Matt become a Christian. Boy, did Matt laugh at that. 'Ain't nobody going to make me become a Christian,' he said."

"I'm sorry." She squeezed his arm.

"He was right. I wasn't trusting God to work in His way and His time. Any more than I was serving Him out of love. God didn't ask me to do things so He had to repay me. He only asks me to serve Him out of love." It had taken him days to come to the conclusion, but when he did, he knew such sweet peace he wondered why he'd fought it so long.

He took Glory's hands in his and faced her full-on. "Glory, I am now free to tell you I love you and want to spend the rest of my life with you at my side."

She studied his features, her gaze searching his eyes, examining his cheeks, his chin, his mouth.

He couldn't read her mind. He feared she was angry at him and couldn't trust him after all the secrets he'd kept.

She lifted her eyes to him. He detected a twinkle in them. "You would marry a woman wearing britches?"

"If you'll have me. I love you, Glory."

Wonderment filled her eyes. "I love you, too. And yes, I'll marry you."

He kissed her smiling mouth. A little later, he told her the rest of it. "I want you to be my partner in every way. My land is your land."

Her eyes widened. "You mean—?"

"Your horses have a home here, too."

"It is more than I asked for or hoped for. God is good."

"He has given us both what our hearts need." Levi kissed her again.

A Letter To Our Readers

Dear Reader:

In order that we might better contribute to your reading enjoyment, we would appreciate your taking a few minutes to respond to the following questions. We welcome your comments and read each form and letter we receive. When completed, please return to the following:

Fiction Editor
Heartsong Presents
PO Box 719
Uhrichsville, Ohio 44683

1. Did you enjoy reading *Glory and the Rawhide Preacher* by Linda Ford?
   ❑ Very much! I would like to see more books by this author!
   ❑ Moderately. I would have enjoyed it more if

   _____

   _____

   _____

2. Are you a member of **Heartsong Presents**? ❑ Yes ❑ No
   If no, where did you purchase this book? _____

   _____

3. How would you rate, on a scale from 1 (poor) to 5 (superior), the cover design? _____

4. On a scale from 1 (poor) to 10 (superior), please rate the following elements.

   ____ Heroine   ____ Plot
   ____ Hero   ____ Inspirational theme
   ____ Setting   ____ Secondary characters

5. These characters were special because? _____

_____

_____

6. How has this book inspired your life? _____

_____

_____

7. What settings would you like to see covered in future
   Heartsong Presents books? _____

_____

_____

8. What are some inspirational themes you would like to see
   treated in future books? _____

_____

_____

9. Would you be interested in reading other **Heartsong
   Presents** titles?   ❑ Yes   ❑ No

10. Please check your age range:
       ❑ Under 18   ❑ 18-24
       ❑ 25-34   ❑ 35-45
       ❑ 46-55   ❑ Over 55

Name _____

Occupation _____

Address _____

City, State, Zip_____

E-mail _____